CRACKED CROAKIES

A MAGICAL COZY MYSTERY WITH TALKING
ANIMALS

SAM CHEEVER

ELECTRIC PROSE PUBLICATIONS

PRAISE FOR SAM CHEEVER

"You have that essential Je ne sais quoi that it takes to tell a story so mesmerizing you cannot stop reading once started. You are not telling stories to your readers...you are taking them with you on your adventures so that the experience can be shared by all as it happens and not simply replayed like a memory on the page of a diary! You are indeed gifted and it is my pleasure to read your books!"

Amazon Reviewer, Valerie Irwin

∾

Croakies has cracked? How is that possible? This is going to be a nightmare if it spreads into the city. I've got to figure out what's going on before that happens, or Croakies isn't going to be the only thing that cracks!

Just when I thought I was starting to hit my stride in this magical artifact librarian gig, everything turns topsy turvy. Several dangerous and toxic artifacts escape from the Powers That Be and one of them lands at Croakies. Because, of course it does. The artifact has cracked Croakies right down the middle and there doesn't seem to be any way to fix it.

In a desperate and potentially deadly move, my crew and I are going on a quest for magical objects that the resident out-of-the-box thinkers believe might seal the crack.

I have no idea if the items will solve our problem. But I'm desperate enough to give it a try.

I only hope we all survive the quest.

STAY IN TOUCH

Sam doesn't give away a lot of books. But she values her readers and, to show it, she's gifting you a copy of a fun book just for signing up for her newsletter!

SIGN UP HERE!
https://samcheever.com/newsletter/

HAPPILY HUNKERED. GREEDILY GATHERED. MUNCHILY MANAGED

"I am thankful," I objected strenuously. Shoving my long, dark brown hair behind my ears, I dared her with my flattest look to deny it.

My opinionated assistant slash friend rolled her iridescent green eyes and plucked the last cookie off the tray my favorite human customer had dropped off only an hour previous. Mrs. Foxladle had been one of my best customers at the bookstore since I'd become Keeper of the Artifacts, and she made truly stupendous turkey-shaped frosted ginger cookies too.

I wet a finger and ran it over the remaining crumbs on the tray. "I only asked what happened to all the cookies? There were three dozen of them when she gave them to me."

The sprite glared in my direction, clearly blaming me for whatever force of nature had swept past the tray and obliterated its abundance. Her narrow freckled face was formed into a dry expression, the look too stern to go with the party-like hues of her fire-red hair and neon green dress. "Hobs is what happened. He and Baca would eat the furniture if it was made from sugar."

"If the furniture was made of sugar, we'd be living in a gingerbread house."

"Ha."

I grabbed the tray and headed for the dividing door into the artifact library. "I'll wash this so I can give it back to her when she comes in to get her books."

Sebille ignored me. She was staring at the floor with a confused expression.

"What's wrong?" I asked.

"Nothing. I just dropped my notebook."

Sure enough, there was a notebook on the floor, the lined pages covered in Sebille's scrawly script.

I clasped the door handle and stopped, turning back to ask, "What's in that notebook anyway? You've been slaving away on it for weeks."

The sprite sent me a fresh glower and bent to snatch it up. "None of your business."

My brows flew skyward. I sensed a prime opportunity to tease the cranky sprite. "It's not a diary, is it?"

Sebille's upper lip curled and vibrated.

Widening my blue eyes, I barked out a laugh. "Are you growling at me?"

"Of course not. Didn't you say you had something you needed to do?"

I tugged on the door and it stuck for a beat before coming open. I'd have to oil the hinges or something. It was starting to get cold outside and everything was sticking. "Lea's supposed to stop by with a basket of apples," I reminded her. "We're making apple pies for Thanksgiving. You're going to help, right?"

The sprite grumbled a response so indistinguishable it

might as well have been composed from ancient Sumerian. I nodded. "Good talk. I'll take that as a yes."

Twenty minutes later, when Sebille and I were sitting companionably at the bookstore table reading, something thumped against the front door. The thump was followed by a cry of pain and the sound of a second impact. Sebille and I shared a look, and I hurried toward the door. Yanking it open, I found my bestie, Leandra Coleman, earth witch extraordinaire, sprawled over the concrete sidewalk, surrounded by apples.

"Lea!" I reached down and grabbed her under the arms. "What happened? Are you okay?"

Shoving wavy light brown hair off her round face, Lea flapped her hands in the air. "I'm fine. I can get up by myself. I just tripped over something." Despite her dismissal of my help, her turquoise gaze was narrowed with worry.

Sebille appeared in the doorway behind me. Her freckled face was pinched in a frown...not an unusual circumstance...and her chin jutted forcefully. "Something's different," she said, her tone filled with mystery.

"What's different is that fresh new crack running from Croakies' front door to the street," Lea said, giving in and taking my hand. Climbing to her feet, she brushed dust off the bum of her frilly, ankle-length skirt and grimaced, carefully working her elbow. "I swear I lifted my foot over it, but somehow it snagged me anyway." Lea sighed. "I think I'm getting old."

Since she was only a few years older than my thirty-two years, that statement was ridiculous.

I plucked two apples off the pavement and put them back into the basket they'd fallen out of. "That crack's been there forever. It must be growing. I'll call the city and make them fix it. Obviously it's become a hazard."

"Has it?"

Lea and I both turned to Sebille. She was leaning against the door jam, skinny, freckled arms crossed over her flat chest. The sprite was staring at the crack, her expression sour.

"Has it what?" I asked, fighting for calm. I swear the sprite was just getting weirder by the day. And she had a secret she was holding closer than a street dog held a discarded bagel. I needed to wrangle that secret out of her before she drove me totally mad with her mysterious attitude.

"*Has* the crack been there for a while?" she asked. "I just noticed it yesterday."

I frowned. "Yeah. I'm pretty sure it's been there since the Spring thaw a couple of years ago." Or maybe it had been only one Spring... I shrugged. "Long enough. I should have already called somebody about it." I winced as Lea examined her torn and bloody elbow. Her pretty pink sweater was ruined. "I'm so sorry. I'll buy you a new sweater. Do you still feel up to baking?"

"Don't be silly. This wasn't your fault. I'm clumsy." Lea shook her head, her hair dancing around her face. The loose waves were glossy and perfect as usual.

I fought the urge to shove my messy dark brown hair into some kind of order and bent to help her pick up the rest of the apples. When we'd gathered them all, we turned toward the door to find Sebille still staring into space. "What *is* your deal, sprite!" I asked, my temper flaring.

Sebille blinked, fixing an unnaturally bright green gaze on me. "Huh?"

"Why are you so spacy?" Then I had a thought and reined in the irritation. "Are you feeling okay?"

She blew a raspberry. "I'm fine. Why wouldn't I be fine? Gators' garters, Naida. Mind your own beeswax, will ya?"

She spun on a shiny red, Wicked Witch of the West, heel and stalked back inside, closing the door in my face. I turned to Lea. "She's up to something. I wish I knew what it was because it's making me very nervous."

Lea linked her arm with mine. "Let's go make some pies. We'll bake an extra little zing into them this year for our human friends."

I opened the door and let her precede me inside. "Did you get pixie honey?"

"I did." Her turquoise eyes widened with pleasure. "The pixies have been happily dusting the flowers the bees visit the most. A slice of this pie will make Mrs. Foxladle feel twenty years younger and put a spring in her step."

I grinned at the thought. Lea had come up with the idea to gift pixed pies to our human friends for Thanksgiving. Like me, she had several loyal non-magical customers who'd been coming into her magical herb shop for years, and we'd been trying to think of a way to thank them.

Pixed pies would be perfect. They'd make our favorite humans feel good and were perfectly harmless.

I held the door for Lea, carefully eyeing her and noting a slight limp. "Are you sure you still want to do this?"

She slid her gaze toward Croakies' second story window, and nodded. "Trust me, this is the right time."

I narrowed my gaze on her. "What did you do?"

Sebille wandered out of the tea area with a steaming cup, blowing to cool the hot liquid. "Does it have anything to do with the fact that I haven't seen the Baked Invaders for several minutes?"

Lea giggled at the name. "Baked Invaders...I see what

you did there. And, yes. The hobgoblin and the brownie are temporarily transfixed."

"Transfixed?" I asked, slightly concerned. "Please clarify."

"They're happily hunkered. Greedily gathered. Munchily managed."

"Surprisingly, I don't feel like that clarified anything."

"She's trying to tell you that she put them in a void bubble."

My eyes went wide as Lea nodded. I must have looked appalled because she flung up her hands. "Before you lose your cool, Naida, they're thoroughly safe and stupendously happy."

"Am I the only one who thinks the witch joined a 'Word of the Day' program?" Sebille snarked.

Lea expelled air. "I filled the bubble with sweets and video games. They'll never want to leave."

"Until they have to pee or something," I grumbled.

Lea grinned. "Slimy's at my place too. I'll send him back when I go home."

I opened my mouth to ask and then slammed it closed. "Never mind. I don't want to know. I just won't look a gift horse in the mouth. Let's bake."

FOUR HOURS LATER, Lea and I had ten apple pies cooling on racks in my little kitchen. We were enjoying a cup of tea and a cookie, with our aching feet elevated. "I can't believe we did ten pies," I told Lea.

She nodded and stretched her feet in front of her, rotating them at the ankles. "We could have done more. I was going to bring some peaches too, but something happened to the tree overnight."

I straightened in my chair. "What happened? Are the peaches ruined?" I loved Lea's fairy-touched peaches almost more than I loved her apples.

"I'm not sure. It just fell over. Queen Sindra has the fairies working on it now."

"Has this happened before?" I turned as a gray slash of fur leaped onto my bed. My magical cat, Mr. Wicked and his littermate and best friend Hex, who belonged to Lea, were leaping and batting at the empty air above the bed. What were those goofy cats up to?

"No," Lea responded, scooping up her cat. Hex gave a plaintive yowl and tried to escape the witch's determined grip. "The rest of the garden seems okay, so I'm just thinking something ate into the roots." She shook her head. "I haven't seen Sindra this mad before. She can't believe something would dare to nibble her perfect trees. Trust me, she'll get to the bottom of it."

The fairy queen, who also happened to be Sebille's mother, took her garden very seriously. It was her kingdom. Her empire. If some hapless bug crawled onto the rich dirt of her garden and gnawed on the tender roots of her prized fruit trees, she'd have that intruder caught and punished to within an inch of its life faster than I could say, Bibbidy-Bobbidi-Boo. "Good. If you need to make jelly or something with the peaches before they go to waste, I'll help."

Lea pushed to her feet. "Thanks, Naida. I'll let you know. Now, I'd better get home and feed my little darling before she finds a way to break into the void and steal the monsters' snacks."

My eyes went wide. "The kids! Do you think they're still in there?"

Lea's gaze slid to the spot in the air that Wicked was slashing with his claws. "They're still in there."

I gave a jolt. "Wait. That's not..."

Lea chuckled. "The void will disintegrate when I leave. I'll send Slimy back in a temperature-controlled bubble. Look for him at your front door in five minutes."

"Wait," I said, stopping her. "You never told me what the fat squish was doing over there."

"Oh." Lea grinned. "He's teaching Wally the alphabet."

"Wally's still alive?" I snapped my mouth closed as I realized how bad that sounded. "I mean. He's not magical, right?" Wally was a bullfrog that had ended up at Lea's place when we'd been trying to help our friend, Rustin find a way back to corporality...long story. We'd been told the frog was magical, but it turned out he was just a normal frog. "How long do bullfrogs live?"

She headed toward the door with her cat in her arms. Hex was still fighting to escape. "I have no idea. But he might have some magic in him after all. I need to go, Naida. I'll tell you about it later." With a wave of her hand toward the spot where Wicked was still swiping his paws at nothing, she left, quietly closing the door behind her.

A magical expulsion of air whooshed through the room, blowing my hair back as a hobgoblin, a brownie, and a cute little green dog appeared out of nowhere and bounced onto my bed. They giggled as a shower of glossy candy wrappers and empty chip bags sifted down on top of them.

The hobgoblin hit the mattress hard and bounced back up, doing a somersault in the air before hitting the bed once more. Baca hit the bed on her hands and did a perfect backspring before landing on her feet.

Vel dove nose-first into my pillows, burrowing into them with happy snorts, and shoving them to the floor.

"Again!" Hobs yelled, ever the daredevil with masochistic tendencies.

"Again!" Baca echoed in her soft, enthusiastic voice.

"Woof!" said my little demon dog Vel, who was generally up for anything anybody wanted to do.

"I can't believe Lea gave you guys all these snacks." I hurried over and started picking up wrappers. "Help me clean this up," I told the trio. But they weren't listening. Before I could make a dent in the detritus from what looked like a week's worth of sugary snacks, Hobs' pale blue gaze suddenly went wide and his nose twitched. "I smell something sweet."

I stiffened, my hands dropping the trash as a flash of panic swept through me.

The pies!

We'd left them cooling on the counter and unleashed the Baked Invaders on the room!

2

HOLY BAT BOOGERS

The thing you might not know about hobgoblins is that they'd do anything for sweets. Anything. And their love of the stuff didn't seem to have any limits. A human type person's "cravings" for sugar paled in comparison to what we'd been dealing with in Hobs. And his brownie girlfriend, Baca wasn't much better.

Between the two of them, they were like locusts in a field of baked goods. By the time I'd realized the mistake Lea and I had made, it was already too late. My head whipped around and I eyed the pies, wondering if I could cross the distance and throw my body over them before the hobgoblin got there.

Not a chance.

Hobs was springing off the bed, his tongue swiping across his thin lips.

Baca wasn't far behind him, her brown eyes glittering.

I may have whimpered

Those pies were toast.

Spinning, I lunged for their skinny legs, knowing I'd be too late. "Vel!" I screamed in sheer desperation.

A deep, power-filled woof blossomed on the air, the notes elongated to the point of being almost unrecognizable. But the magic in Vel's bark kicked in and the world slowed, oozing like molasses as I watched the scene unfold at a severely decelerated speed.

Across the room, the door slowly opened, and Lea's wild-eyed face appeared. Beside her, caught in a time-delayed spring from Lea's arms, Hex hung in the air with her mouth open on an irritated yowl.

"Theeeeeee piiiiiiiiies!" Lea said, her voice unnaturally lengthened through time.

Hobs stretched his long limbs in preparation for a magically-enhanced sprint and I had a sudden vision of being the Wile E. Coyote to his Road Runner. Even locked within Vel's speed-constrained magic, he looked as if he'd be faster than I was. On my other side, Baca's tiny face turned oh so slowly toward mine, her brown eyes wide and her lips curving in a triumphant smile.

I was going to lose the race. The pies we'd spent hours baking would disappear in a blur of movement that would be too fast for me to witness.

Across the room, something long, rubbery, and charcoal-gray undulated away from Lea's outstretched fingers and I watched hopefully as the void bubble crept toward its target. The magical construct would keep the pies safe if we could get there in time. Even as I stretched further, I called Vel's name again, hoping the little demon dog would understand my unspoken request.

Like a pimple popping beneath a determined fingernail, the air around me gave a soft little "pop" and I was suddenly free of the morass. I surged forward, my fingers closing around the two miscreants and holding fast as they nearly pulled me off my feet.

The void bubble leached forward, achingly slow but already restructuring in size and shape to fit its required load.

Without warning, Hobs' scrawny form gained weight and jerked, nearly breaking loose of my hold.

I gave a surprised little scream that exploded into the distorted space around me like a firecracker. The naughty little hobgoblin was all but free, with only my desperately clutching fingertips still keeping him back.

I gritted my teeth, watching the void ooze toward the pies. Closer, but not close enough.

With another jolt, Hobs was free. "Hobs, no," I screamed.

The air swirled and he was suddenly standing over the pies, his long, spidery fingers curving toward them.

A yowl.

A jolt in the molasses air.

A gray blur flew past. Wicked slammed into Hobs, taking him to the ground, their fall caught in the ooze of time.

The moment reasserted itself. With a satisfying snap, the void caught up to its target and wrapped around the pies, locking into place and disappearing from sight.

Baca dropped to her feet with a happy squeal and ran for Hobs, leaping into the play as the hobgoblin rolled, giggling on the floor with Mr. Wicked, who was quickly joined by Hex.

Lea and I sagged into the nearest chairs, panting.

That had been way too close.

I opened my mouth to say as much as the entire building gave a violent shudder, followed by a horrendous cracking sound.

Lea and I leaped to our feet and ran toward the door,

skidding to a stop on the small landing as we took in the sight below.

"Holy bat boogers," I mumbled, my heart pounding hard enough to make me dizzy.

Beside me, Lea made a choked sound, her hand reaching blindly for mine. "Naida?"

A prolonged squeal of tortured metal drew our attention to the furthest corner of the artifact library, where one of the massive, floor-to-ceiling shelving units containing hundreds of magical artifacts sat at an odd angle, its frame appearing twisted from where I stood.

"What is...?"

I shook my head, answering the question my bestie seemed unable to finish. "I don't have a clue."

The dividing door between the bookstore and the artifact library slammed back against the wall, and Lea and I jumped, yelping in surprise.

Sebille appeared in the open doorway, her long face suffused with color and her bangs sticking to her glossy forehead. She was panting. "Is everybody all right back here?" She was holding what looked like a pry bar in her freckled hands.

"We're okay," I said, looking down to where Vel plopped on my foot and the two cats wound around our ankles. Hobs and Baca hadn't emerged. "Hobs?"

"Here, miss," he said, his white tunic and matching cotton trousers coloring the blur of his arrival, which was faster than the mind could fathom.

Baca showed up a beat later, her delicately pretty face pink from their play. "Whatever has happened?" the small brownie breathed, her bright brown gaze skimming the massive warehouse space below.

Sebille frowned. "The door wouldn't open. The floor

is..." She looked down to where she straddled a wide crack in the concrete, one 'Wicked Witch of the West' shoe on either side of it. The sprite lifted her gaze to follow the path of the fissure.

It snaked along the center of the entire library, wandering across the concrete floor like a riverbed. Somehow, the crack's path had missed all but the single canted shelf that was still groaning as its metal feet clung precariously to the edge of the crumbling concrete. The width of the fracture varied from a couple of inches in one area, to a spot near the very center of the space that looked to be three feet across.

Dust sifted from the ceiling as if the very bones of the building had been displaced. And a low moan slipped through the space as we stared in awe at the destruction below us.

"Croakies is cracked," Hobs said, his voice breaking against the silence.

Down by my feet Vel whined softly. I cast a speculative glance her way. Had she caused the crack with her bark? The little demon dog's *woof* power was prolific. It was possible the damage to Croakies had come as a side effect of the magic I'd asked her to supply inside my apartment.

She whined again, swiping her tongue over the toe of my sneaker and giving me a sad look.

I crouched down and gave her a hug. "It's not your fault, girl," I told the little dog. "If anything, it's mine. I asked you to do it."

"Do what, miss?" Hobs asked.

I looked into his slightly bulging light blue gaze and considered my next words carefully. Hobs blinked at me, the little tuft of light brown hair between his oversized ears shifting in the air of an overhead fan. Part of me wanted to tell him that his greedy ways had caused too much stress and strain at Croakies lately. To scold him for his part in the current catastrophe. But a larger part of me...the part that was currently tumbling into the soft innocence of his gaze... knew I couldn't do it. "Nothing." I stood up. "We need to figure out why these cracks are happening." I looked at Sebille. "Can you go talk to your mom?"

As evidence of just how spooked the sprite was, she simply nodded and spun on her shiny heel to do as I asked.

I descended the stairs to the warehouse. Standing on the bottom step, I stared at the crack for a long moment. I wasn't confident that it was safe to step onto the floor.

"Here," Lea said, reaching out a hand. "Take my hand and I'll pull you back if the floor gives out beneath you."

I took the offered lifeline and sucked in a deep, bracing breath before touching the floor with a toe. It felt firm. I pressed harder, leaning some of my weight into it. The floor didn't move. I stepped down and waited, the toes of my back foot still on the bottom step.

"Does it feel solid?" Lea asked, her tone hushed.

"So far."

A high-pitched shriek yanked my gaze upward to find the hobgoblin standing on the railing above my head. "Hobs, don't you dare!"

Ignoring me like I wasn't there, he leaped, his spindly form sommersaulting three times before his oversized feet hit the floor with a meaty slap and he straightened proudly. "Score?" he called out.

"Ten!" Baca happily replied.

"Twenty," I unhappily added. "That's how many minutes of time out you're getting for that stunt, young man."

Hob's sunny expression clouded over. "Miss?"

"You and I have had this talk." I crouched down in front

of him. Despite his light-weight, twenty-eight-inch-tall size, he appeared undaunted by my fluffy, five-feet-nine-inch form looming over him. "You're going to run out of luck one of these days and seriously hurt yourself." The tiny creature seemed to have a death wish when it came to stunts and aerial tricks. In recent weeks, his wildness had seemed to triple and he was starting to scare me. "Twenty minutes in your den without snacks, video games, or Baca."

His eyes turned glossy with unshed tears. "But, miss..."

"I'm sorry, Hobs." And I was. For the first time I understood the meaning of the phrase, "this hurts me more than it hurts you."

"You need to think before you do crazy stuff. And..." I added as his oversized ears drooped. "You need to think before eating everything in Croakies. If you can't learn to control your eating so that others in this building can eat too, I'll make a new rule of no snacks allowed at Croakies."

"No, miss," he breathed. The expression of horror on his little face nearly made me smile. He looked as if someone had threatened the life of his favorite pet.

"Believe it or not, you wouldn't die without sweets." Except I wasn't sure about that. Hobgoblins metabolized sugar differently from humans. To them it wasn't extra calories. It was prime calories. I doubted I'd be able to fulfill my threat. But I needed to do something to make him function with more thought and consideration. As he plowed through his teen years, he was fast becoming a liability and if I didn't get him under control, I'd have to do something about it.

I didn't like my choices of things to do.

When I'd decided he could stay at Croakies, I hadn't been thinking about Hobs as a difficult teen. I'd been seeing the small, helpless hobgoblin child who'd needed a home and someone to love him. He still needed those things. But he needed to work with me or we'd have to reconsider if Croakies could be that home.

"Off to your den. I'll see you in twenty minutes."

"Yes, miss." He left in a blur of white, an invisible string tugging painfully at my heart in his wake.

"I can't repair this damage," said a soft voice down by my feet.

I glanced down at Baca. "No?" The brownie could generally fix anything, whether through clever workmanship or magic. She generally made the damaged item even stronger than before it had been broken. It was shocking to hear she didn't view the floor as fixable.

Shaking her head, Baca tucked an escaped strand of brown hair behind one tiny ear. As usual, the two-foot-tall brownie was dressed in a brown tunic and pants, with a tool belt slung around her narrow hips and a fall-colored band holding back her hair. The colors of the hair band changed with the seasons, but generally tended toward warm, earthy colors rather than bright. "This isn't just a physical crack," she said, her voice even softer than usual. "It's an artifact."

I felt my eyes go wide. "The crack is an artifact?"

She nodded, frowning. "I've never seen its like before. I'm not exactly sure how to get rid of it."

"Maybe we can patch it," Lea said from behind me. "Just cover it up."

I twitched in surprise, having momentarily forgotten that she was there.

Baca seemed to give that some thought. After a moment, she shook her head. "I don't think that would work. It would have to be part of the magic. Or, at the very least, a relic that was compatible."

We stood in silence for a beat before I thought to ask the most important question. "Do you think it will grow?"

Baca didn't hesitate. "Yes. It's a living artifact, which means it must grow to survive."

"Whistling warthogs," I breathed. "How on the goddess's green earth did this happen?"

"I take it you didn't get an order to store this artifact at Croakies?" Lea asked.

I shook my head. That was generally how it worked at the artifact library. Whenever the Universal Council or its agents, the Powers That Be rescued or confiscated an artifact from someone who didn't deserve it, became unable to care for it, or couldn't control it, they sent an order for the magical item to me, declaring the need for safe storage at the artifact library. My ability to accept the artifacts had grown with my connection to the library and I rarely missed an order anymore. "I suppose it's possible I missed it, but..." I frowned, not believing that the Council would just fling such a dangerous artifact at me without any warning. But just in case... "I need to speak to Maddie."

Lea nodded. "I thought you might say that. I'm going with you."

3

WELL, I'LL BE A SLUG'S AUNTIE

Contrary to popular opinion around Croakies, I *can* learn a lesson. One of the things I'd learned was never to visit a powerful PTB without an invite. Yes, I'd learned it the hard way. But...whatever. That was why we were calling Maddie on my magical communication mirror rather than just dropping by her castle, which was protected by giant vultures in the heart of the deadly Enchanted Forest.

"Madeline Quilleran, I need to speak with you," I intoned. The glass in the standing mirror swirled with gray mist as I stared into it, knowing I was just as likely to get Maddie's cranky Russian raven familiar as I was to get her.

I braced myself as the mist began to thin and narrowed my gaze on the scene before me. The room looked much as it always had, with copious numbers of rugs scattered over the floor of a massive room whose central feature was a floor-to-ceiling stone fireplace. The hearth was currently dark, the bricks at the back of the oversized fireplace blackened from heavy use.

Leaning against the stone on one end of the mantle, was

a painting of the Enchanted Forest that was so vibrant and multi-dimensional that the dense trees and rich, loamy soil looked real enough to touch. At the other end were three mismatched silver candlesticks, their slightly tarnished forms artfully coated in knotty dribbles of melted and cooled wax.

And above the aged wood mantle...

I jolted, blinking.

"Hello, Naida keeper."

My mouth fell open as I looked into the bright brown gaze of the magical stag head hanging above the hearth.

Felonius generally made a game out of seeing without being seen, his intense gaze seeming to spear me with notice a blink before I turned to find him staring blankly straight ahead. He'd never spoken to me. Never given up the game. Which was why I was shocked to find him addressing me directly. "Felonious. What's wrong? Where's Madeline? Where's Maude?"

The stag's head tipped like a curious bird's. "Why do you assume something is wrong?"

I bristled at his assumption I'd be too dense to recognize what was implied by his breaking protocol. "You wouldn't be talking to me if something hadn't happened. Where are they?"

Felonious sighed. "I'm afraid there's a problem at the Universal Council. One of the members accidentally allowed a particularly dangerous collection of artifacts to escape."

I closed my eyes, realizing that instead of getting help, I was most likely going to be told that I was on my own. I sighed, my eyes coming open. "Ah. Okay. Well, I guess you won't be surprised to hear that one of them landed on my doorstep?" I quickly described the cracking artifact. "Is there anybody who can help me deal with it?"

"All of the PTBs and their assistants are addressing similar issues with degradation artifacts. I've been instructed to tell keepers who called in for help that the council will take their names and get back to them as quickly as possible." The stag's glossy brown gaze tightened. "But, Maddie said not to count on it. These are some of the most dangerous artifacts in existence. It will take all hands on deck to stop them."

I expelled a frustrated breath. "Okay, I'm calling to report that Croakies has cracked. The resident brownie doesn't believe she can seal the fissure and that it will continue to grow. If there's anybody anywhere who has insight on this, I'd greatly appreciate any advice or help I can get."

Felonious dipped his regal head, the overhead lights glinting off his massive rack of antlers. "I'll enter your request into the record." He settled a thoughtful look on me. "How far has the crack traveled?"

"So far it's just inside the artifact library." As soon as I made the statement, I realized it was wrong. "And the bookstore."

The stag winced. "The artifacts are in danger?"

"Yes. We'll try to move the ones in its path, but if it keeps growing..."

He sighed, the sound strange coming from the magical head. "As bad as it is having the toxic artifact in the library, you don't want it to get loose on Enchanted City's streets, Naida keeper. Mundanes have no protection against this type of artifact. It will consume and kill everything in its path."

"And nobody can tell me how to stop it? How is that possible?"

He shook his antlers, somehow avoiding clanking them against the wall. "One of the reasons these artifacts are so dangerous is because the protocols for dealing with them were destroyed a millennia ago by the trickster who set them loose."

"*Well, I'll be a slug's auntie,*" I mumbled. Dang tricksters were always causing trouble.

"If anything changes, please make sure to inform me," Felonious said, clearly dismissing me.

Disconnecting after promising that I'd keep him informed, I covered the mirror with the protective shroud we'd started using after a doppelganger infected Croakies' mirrors in an attempt to gain control over me.

"We're on our own?" Lea asked softly.

I nodded, my hands still resting on the covered mirror. "I'm going to need to do a lot of research."

Lea nodded. "I'll go through all my grimoires. Maybe there's something witchy I can do to help."

"Thanks, Lea."

My friend patted my arm and hurried out of the library. A moment later I heard the jangle of the doorbell as she exited the store.

When it jangled again sometime later, I was perched on the steps leading up to my apartment, staring hopelessly at the crack. I hadn't had much luck researching the artifact, and my misery was growing as I stared at it, convinced it was getting bigger by the moment.

Apparently, when the protocols for dealing with the artifacts had been destroyed, all documentation about them had also been lost.

A deep, familiar voice called out from inside the bookstore. "Naida?"

"Back here." I slumped. Even the sound of my sweetie pie's sexy voice didn't perk me up.

Grym poked his dark head through the dividing door, his gaze narrowing when he saw me sitting there. "Hey. You okay? You look a little spooked."

Standing at just under six feet tall with broad shoulders, dark-caramel eyes, and mahogany brown hair that was brightened by natural golden streaks where the sun had bleached it, my sweetie was pure eye candy. When you added his sexy square jaw and cheek bones that could have been carved from stone, he was irresistible. A sight for sore eyes. But even he couldn't bring a smile to my lips.

"I am spooked." Nodding toward the long crack down the middle of the library, I said, "Apparently this is an artifact and nobody knows how to stop it."

He moved into the room, muscles bunching nicely as he crouched beside the fissure and carefully checked it out. When he reached toward the crack, I panicked. "Don't touch it!"

Grym blinked at me in surprise. "It's okay, Naida. It won't do anything to me."

"We don't know that," I told him. I stood up and moved closer, until I stood across the crack from him. "I know rock is impervious to most things. But cracks aren't one of those things." And since Grym was mostly rock in his supernormal form, that made my new fixture extremely dangerous to him.

Grym's chin lifted, his eyes darkening as he either considered arguing with me or, more likely, suddenly realized how serious my problem was.

I understood his frustration. Grym was tough and smart. He was also a cop for the supernormal branch of the Enchanted Police Department, a team that much of the police force and the population of Enchanted City were unaware existed. To most of the people he bumped up against, Grym was just a detective. A cop. And he *was* that. But he was also a gargoyle. Given that gargoyles are all about protecting things, he was a natural for his job. Being built of rock in his supernormal form, Grym was used to being impervious to almost everything. Usually, he was a big help when I came up against a toxic artifact. But he would be just as vulnerable as the rest of us to the rogue magic that was currently attacking Croakies.

"Did you contact Maddie?"

I nodded. "There's not going to be any help coming from the PTBs or the Council." I told him what the stag had told me. "And the brownie can't do anything with it either."

He sat back on his haunches, one hand dangling off his knee as he eyed the artifact. "If it's a magical problem, you're going to need magic to fix it."

I bit back the urge to say, "Duh."

But when he glanced back at me, he must have seen the reaction in my face. He smiled. "What I mean is, there's no point looking at mundane ways to fix this. No physical fix will help. This is a job strictly for the supernormal world. And mostly those with Earth magic."

I saw what he was saying. My talent pool was going to be small. "Witches and fairies."

"Ogres and rock trolls."

I blinked. "Huh?"

"Who knows more about rocky cracks and crevices than ogres and trolls?"

Nodding, I said, "right." King Rhorr's kingdom was built on a rocky landscape. The ogres lived in caves and cherished their harsh surroundings. Queen Kaith of the rock trolls would be my second choice for an ally. The common trolls lived in caves, but Kaith's queendom was mostly grassy meadow and she lived in a glass and metal castle in the center of it. She was less likely to be able or willing to help. And she was a scary critter. Much meaner than the ogre king by far.

"We have more options than I'd thought we would," I told Grym.

"As long as we keep all of our allies away from each other so we don't start a supernormal war."

He smiled and I grinned back. "I'll let you do the negotiating with King Rhorr," I teased. "It didn't work out so well the last time I did it."

That was a vast understatement. Sebille and I had somehow missed the small print in the ogres' extensive contract and had ended up affianced to two of the ogres. It had taken a whole mess of plans and situations to get us out of that one.

I wasn't risking that again.

"You're right," Grym said, kissing my forehead. "We can't risk another inopportune affiancing. I sort of have designs on you myself."

Despite my poor mood, my lips curved into a goofy smile. "Is that even a word?"

"Affiancing? Who knows? But you knew what I meant, right?"

"I did." Pleasure continued to warm my belly and decorate my face. "No affiancing to ogres for me."

"Right. Now, where do you want to go first?"

4

I'VE BEEN LOOKING ALL OVER
FOR THIS

Maybe it was cowardly of me to go to the easiest target first. But...well...it was only marginally easy in a list of impossible tasks so maybe I could be forgiven for it.

Finding myself, once again, stumbling over the rocky landscape of King Rhorr's kingdom was surreal. The last time I'd been there, I'd been terrified of losing my friends and being forced into an unacceptable pairing.

Hopefully, the current visit would be better.

I barely had time to register the wall of hot pink before it slammed into me, sending me stumbling several feet before the dense squishiness of too much flesh encircled my waist to keep me from sailing away.

Grym had time to say, "Ah..." before another wall of flesh slammed into me from the other side, followed by a gruff chorus of giggling.

I didn't panic as I inhaled the flowery sweetness of the ogres' scent. It wasn't my first rodeo in Ogreville. "Hey, Rish. Hey, Mmphine." My poor squished face couldn't quite pronounce their names right.

More giggling preceded a squishy rocking motion as the two oversized creatures did a little lullaby dance with me in the center.

My face and hands were all that stuck out from the two slices of ogre bread in the Naida sandwich. And my cheeks were squished like a toddler's face between an over exuberant aunt's pinching fingers.

"Naida keeper!" they chorused enthusiastically, bouncing on their big, flat feet. Sticking out in front of me, my arms bounced with them. Sweat ran down my sides from being enveloped in their cushiony heat. "Cabn dyou guysh let bme go dnow?"

"Oh!" exclaimed the hot pink wall of flesh. "Did I break her again?"

The lime green wall shimmied as I envisioned Rick shaking his oversized head. "No. She's fine. Humans aren't big huggers I think."

"Ah..." Grym tried again.

"Dthat's Grybm," I said, trying to smile. Unfortunately, my puckered fishy lips wouldn't stretch that way. "He'th bmy boyfriend."

The two ogres exclaimed and started dancing again, singing, "Naida has a boyfriend. Naida has a boyfriend."

Had I really thought the ogres would be the easiest allies to deal with?

"Nice to meet you," Grym said, offering them his hand. Unlike mine, Grym's big hand didn't look like a toddler's in the ogres' big paws. But it did look like an adolescent's. "Maybe you could let her breath now?" he suggested blandly.

"Oh!" Maxine and Rick both jumped back at the same time, leaving me wobbling at the sudden loss of support. I tipped forward, arms cartwheeling and Maxine's huge hand flashed out to smack me on the forehead. I was pretty sure the intention had been to readjust my tilt, but all it did was send me flying backward to smack into the ground. I lay there, seeing stars and birdies circling my head as she bounced around me in horror. "I broke her! I broke her! I always break her."

I groaned, not even trying to rise. Why bother? The ogres would only knock me down again.

"Maybe you could step back?" Grym said, moving his big body toward them, forcing them to move unless they wanted to chest bump with him.

Rick and Maxine complied, but just barely. I could feel their excitement throbbing in the air.

Grym smiled at me as he pulled me to my feet, brushing rock dust off my back. "You okay?"

"Good," I said, eyeing Maxine as she twitched uncertainly. She made a move as if to grab me again and my hands flew up in an obvious defensive maneuver. Maxine frowned.

Like the other times I'd seen them, the pair were wearing short shorts and belly-baring tee-shirts over their brightly-hued forms. Rick had cut his white beard since I'd last seen him, but he still looked a lot like Hreck of human movie fame, except he didn't have the horn-shaped ears and his face was more angular, with high, sharp cheekbones and a broad chin. The bright green color of his eyes was a few shades darker than his vivid skin but not as bright as Sebille's iridescent green gaze.

Rick had a wisp of a white beard that ran from just under his wide lips to below his cleft chin and an abundance of white hair that covered his broad head. The rest of his enormous form appeared to be completely hairless.

In contrast, Maxine's dense wave of golden hair hung to

her slanted shoulders and flipped up at the ends. Her eyes were a deep pink, basically purple. Unlike Rick, she had a thick forest of golden hair along her forearms and from her knees down. Her massive belly was bare and sans hair. "It's really nice to see you both again," I said to soften my defensiveness. "Are you well?"

Rick nodded enthusiastically. "I'm good. The king is letting me marry my sweet Delphia."

"That's good news," I exclaimed.

"And I'm being allowed to pursue my career as kingdom librarian," Maxine said, clapping her meaty hands. "Life is beautiful."

I couldn't help sharing her grin. I'd come to realize that the two were not typical ogres. I thought they might be very young, maybe mid-to-late teens. And their enthusiasm was both catching and dangerous.

"Why are you here?" Rick asked.

"We need to speak to the king," I told him. "Is he available?"

"WAIT HERE," Rick told us, indicating we should stand a few feet away from the swirling vortex that formed the entrance to King Rhorr's throne room. Grym and I shared a look as Maxine waved gaily at other ogres around the rocky compound. In many ways, the pink-hued young ogre seemed to have matured since I'd last seen her. She seemed bigger for one thing, and had more confidence than she'd had before. Judging by the number of ogres who called out greetings to her while we waited, she was also very popular.

Curious gazes skimmed over us and, in some cases, blatantly hostile ones. There were some who blamed us for the death of one of their elders when an evil piper entered Rhorr's kingdom months earlier, and still others resented the fact that Sebille and I had refused to allow ourselves to be added to Rhorr's trophy wall through marriage.

A particularly large ogre strode toward us across the compound, his beady red eyes fixed with more than a little hostility as he glowered toward Grym. I wondered if it was one of the ones Grym had battled before. I admitted to myself that I couldn't tell. It wasn't that all ogres looked alike. They certainly didn't. But that had been a stressful time for me, and I had a feeling I'd been viewing the altercation through a truncated lens.

"Grym," I said softly.

"I see him," he said, turning toward the oncoming threat and stepping in front of me.

"I don't want you to fight," I told him, placing a hand on his arm, which was so tense it felt as if it had already turned to rock.

"Tell *him* that," he growled. His voice also sounded gravely. He was seconds away from going gargoyle on me. While that form would give him the best chance of survival against one of the massive ogres, it would also be seen as aggression, and responded to as such.

I did the only thing I could do under the circumstances. I stepped around Grym, holding up my hands. "Stop! We're here to speak with the king. He won't be pleased if you kill us before we can tell him about a danger to his kingdom."

Ogres wandered out of caves all around us. Curious gazes turned to anger in some, and worry in others. My tension ratcheted up a few notches. The last thing we needed was for them to gang up on us. "Grym, we have more company."

If the ogre heard anything I said, he showed no signs.

Only six feet away from us, he reached a long arm shaped like a battering ram toward me and growled, long and low. Hot spittle splattered my face.

Grym leaped in front of me, his clothing tearing as the change came over him.

"No!" I yelled as the two men crashed into each other. Massive, block-like fists swung and connected, the sound like two boulders crashing together at the end of a rockslide.

The ogre stumbled backward two steps, but quickly regained his balance and leaned into his next punch. The punch took Grym right off his feet and slammed him into the rocky bluff behind us.

Stones as big as my fists rolled down the wall, barely missing Grym's large, blocky form and skittering across the hard dirt with a soft clatter. Grym shoved upright, his gargoyle form much more agile than it should be, and his tenacity exactly what you'd expect from a man made of rock.

The ogre met him in the middle, smashing his torso into Grym's charging form and meeting resistance as my gargoyle dug in with his massive feet and leaned into the attack.

Grym jerked his head forward, butting the ogre in the forehead and then following it up with a one-two punch to his kidneys.

The ogre grunted and tensed, pain sliding through his strange, dark eyes as he lifted a massive leg and stomped Grym's foot.

Hard flesh slammed against rock-like limbs. Grunts grew into shouts. Bodies flailed and surged, kicking up dirt and rocks until I was sneezing from all the dust.

Blood-smeared faces and fists flashed, almost too quickly for me to follow. I thought Grym was holding his own...even seemed to be coming out a little ahead. He presented a quick burst of punches that had the ogre stumbling backward, his hands coming up in a defensive stance.

Then I heard another growl of rage and tore my gaze from the two combatants to find two more ogres striding quickly forward.

"Grym!" I screamed, looking around for something to use as a weapon. My only inherent defensive skill was through magical artifacts. If I tried to douse the ogres with keeper magic, they'd only pee their pants or get curly hair.

Not very useful in a fight.

I suddenly wished I'd thought to bring Blackbeard's sword with me. But I'd hoped I wouldn't need it.

Throwing myself between the two newcomers, I flung up my hands. "No! Stay out of this."

Their only response was a chuckle that sounded like pebbles rolling downhill.

In desperation, I threw out a hand and sent my keeper's magic outward. If there was an artifact nearby it would hopefully come to me.

The two pressed forward, the green ogre shoving a massive hand against my shoulder, flinging me to the ground. I landed on sharp pieces of rock and winced at the pain. "We just want to speak to King Rhorr!" I yelled in desperation.

The other newcomer, an ogre with midnight skin, punched Grym in the kidney. The gargoyle rammed his granite fist into the guy's gut, kicking the second one on the side of the knee as the charcoal gray attacker lunged. It didn't stop the ogre from wrapping long, thick fingers around Grym's throat.

"Stop that!" I surged to my feet and pounded on the one closest to me. The green ogre swung at me but I ducked and he missed. I stomped on his foot and yelped as my own foot twanged with pain.

The gray ogre growled and slammed a fist into Grym's side.

Grym didn't react, though the maneuver had to be incredibly painful. He kept punching, his big form slanting toward the other man, and the force of his response driving him back.

There was a soft hiss of air behind me and I turned to find Maxine missing. She must have gone through the portal to inform Rhorr of the battle.

I panicked. The last thing we needed was to enrage the ogre king. We needed his help. We didn't need to have him throw us out of the compound for causing trouble. "Grym! The King."

Grym was too busy to notice my call of warning.

The portal hissed again.

I turned to find a tall figure with a mop of messy white hair and small, hard eyes below bushy white brows striding out of the swirling vortex. King Rhorr wore his customary velvet robe with white fur on the lapel and encircling the sleeves and hem.

He didn't look happy.

The air above my head whispered and my hand shot up, fingers closing over the artifact that had answered my call.

A writing quill.

Buffalo boogers! Just once I'd like to be lucky enough to get a real weapon instead of a harmless piece of fluff.

"Desist!" the king roared, his voice an explosion on the air.

The combatants all jerked to a stop and stiffened, their gazes lowering and their chins drooping to their chests.

Grym stood in the center of the ogres, eyes flashing and

chest heaving from exertion. Even in his current disheveled state, I'd recognize the lines of my boyfriend's square chin and strong features anywhere.

He dipped his head, ever the diplomat. When he spoke, he wasn't even breathless. "Your Majesty."

The king strode forward, hand outstretched as he came even with me, and snatched the quill from my grip. "I've been looking all over for this," the king of the ogres said. Rhorr arched a dense white brow at me, humor sparkling in his bright blue, beadlike eyes. "Thank you for finding it."

I gave a half-hearted, ha, ha, ha, and he turned toward Grym. "Detective Grym. You're out of uniform."

Grym's "uniform" was currently in tatters on the dusty ground. His denim shirt had been trampled in the melee and his jeans, though still clinging to his hips and thighs, hung in ribbons over his calves. "Just getting a little exercise with your subjects," Grym said, keeping a straight face.

The ogres shuffled their massive feet and grunted.

Rhorr turned a hard glance on his men. "Back to your caves. And don't leave them until I send someone to get you."

All three ducked their heads and turned swiftly, striding away toward the rocky ridge where most of them had their homes. Rhorr sighed. "I apologize. I'm afraid hard feelings take time to soften."

I nodded. "We understand, Majesty."

Rhorr motioned toward the vortex. "Come. I've had libations set out. We'll eat and drink, and you can tell me why you're here."

5

HAVE YOU NOT MET AELICE?

I held a cookie in my hand that felt as if it weighed five pounds and was hard enough to chip my teeth. Neither Grym nor King Rhorr seemed to have any trouble eating the things, and both had gone back for thirds. I'd been lucky to get away with nibbling the rigid edge whenever Rhorr glanced my way. I'd even tried dunking it in the lukewarm tea I'd been given but that hadn't done a thing to soften it. Deciding to stuff it into my pocket when the king wasn't looking, I could only hope it didn't weigh me down on the trek back to Croakies.

"Tell me what has you desperate enough to return to us," Rhorr said, his blue bead eyes twinkling with good humor. The first time I'd seen the ogre king, he'd reminded me of a Bad Santa. Seeing him twinkle at me only cemented that earlier impression. "You *are* aware there are other unattached males in my kingdom I could affiance to you?"

I forced a smile and palmed the cookie, folding my hands together over it and placing them in my lap. "I'll have to pass, King Rhorr." I glanced at Grym. "I'm already with someone."

Rhorr lowered his bushy white brows at Grym and made a chuffing sound. "Yes. That's unfortunate. But it's clear you enjoy a man with a rocky disposition. If you ever find yourself in need of a new one..."

Grym coughed into his hand, clearly hiding a smile.

I glowered at him. "That may be sooner than you think," I mumbled softly. In a louder voice I said, "I'm afraid something's happened and we're all in danger." As the humor fled the king's gaze, I told him about the five escaped toxic artifacts and gave detail on the one that we'd "found" at Croakies.

When I'd finished, Rhorr nodded his big head. "I shall send you my Rock Meister. She will get to the bottom of things." He winked. "So to speak."

"Rock Meister?" I asked, frowning.

"Yes." His brow furrowed. "Have you not met Aelice?"

"I haven't had the pleasure, sire."

"Ah." He barked out a laugh. "You're in for a treat then." He leaned close and lowered his voice. "Whatever you do, do not come to an accord with her. She's wily, that one."

I felt my eyes going wide. But before I could ask any questions, Rhorr went on. "We can handle the transaction with a standard contract. There should be nothing in it to concern anyone." He lifted a hand and Rick ambled over with a scroll.

Grym cleared his throat. "With all due respect, Your Majesty, Naida isn't signing a contract today. This danger will affect us all. If you don't help us stop it, there's a good chance some of the toxic magic will find its way to your kingdom. Your people are in danger."

Rhorr's brow puckered. "No contract? That's not possible. I must have something in writing."

I shrugged, standing. "I'm sorry we couldn't come to an agreement."

Grym stood too. He sighed. "I'm not looking forward to our next visit."

I shook my head. "Me neither."

Rhorr perked up. "Next visit?"

"If you won't work with us, we'll need to go to Queen Kaith." I let that hang there between us for a moment. I figured the king would react in a minute or two, but it only took fifteen seconds.

"I can do this without a contract. Just this once."

"Good," Grym said, his handsome face showing no sign of the smugness I knew he was feeling. It had been his idea to use the troll queen as a pressure point in our negotiations with Rhorr. The two rulers had enjoyed a long, intense competition that I wasn't sure was purely professional. "We look forward to meeting with the Meister."

"Yes," Rhorr said, his gaze narrowing suspiciously. But he took Grym's hand, pumping it as if he were a jack for a car. "May our venture prove successful in a prompt and satisfying fashion."

"Yes," I said, agreeing as Rhorr turned my way.

When he reached for my hand, I panicked. I still had the cookie clutched there. But Rhorr grinned, turning his hand over and wiggling his fingers.

I sighed and gave up the goods, dropping it into his huge paw. "Rock biscuits are not for everyone." He clacked his teeth together. "You need strong choppers."

"Ha," I said, feeling self-conscious at having been caught. "Thanks for hearing us out, King Rhorr. If your rock...erm...Meister can help us, that would be amazing."

"I am certain she can. Look for her in the next day or so.

In the meantime," He glanced past us, to where Rick and Maxine stood in front of the portal.

They dropped to one knee and lowered their heads, speaking in unison. "Sire?"

"Accompany the keeper and her detective off the compound. I don't believe there will be any more incidents, but better safe than sorry."

"Of course, sire," they responded.

They stood and Rick preceded us through the portal. Maxine ushered us out after him and followed on our heels.

We'd nearly reached the edge of Rhorr's kingdom before I had a chance to break into the ogres' running commentary to ask about the Meister.

"Aelice?" Rick asked. "She's a wily one."

I winced. Clearly the Meister's tricky personality was universally known and accepted. Unfortunately, that was the last thing I wanted to deal with given the circumstances.

CROAKIES WAS CLOSED and nobody greeted us as we came through the door.

Well...nobody human.

It's about time. What's it gonna take for a guy to get a few crickets here?

I glanced toward the glass tank on the short wall across from the sales counter. The fat green squish with bulging eyes gave a little hop when we noticed him, his throat swelled into a *Ribbit* as if to emphasize his desperation.

"Sebille didn't feed you?" I set my purse down on the table a little harder than necessary. My assistant knew it was her job to feed the frog. A sacred duty, because if we didn't feed him on a timely basis, there was holy heartache suffered by one and all.

The squish made sure of it.

I dumped some crickets into his glass home and pulled the dish we used for his "pond" out to give him fresh warm water.

Cheh!

I stopped midway to the sink and looked at Slimy. "Was that a cough?"

No...cheh...I'm not sick. Cheh.

I looked at Grym. He frowned. "That was a cough."

I filled the pond with warm water and carried it back to the aquarium, settling it back into place beneath the heat lamp.

I lowered my face toward the frog. "Did you choke on a cricket?" Grimacing at the bug leg sticking out of his mouth, I reached to put a finger on his forehead.

His skin felt cool to the touch. Which meant nothing. "Do you feel sick?"

I'm not sick. I'm splendiferous. The frog gave a little hop as if to prove that he was as good as gold. Then he coughed.

"What did I tell you about playing with the thesaurus?" I asked him, smiling.

I'm growing my vocabulary. What's wrong with that?

"What's wrong is that you stab me in the psyche with every new word you learn. They're not growth, they're weapons."

The frog slurped up another cricket. I looked away. I'd never get used to that.

Drama much! he accused, then succumbed to a barrage of coughing, topped off with a sneeze.

"You're sick!" Alarm made my stomach twist. I turned a horrified gaze to Grym. "He's sick."

Always calm in a crisis, Grym coolly walked over and stared down at the frog. "Maybe we should take his temperature."

Ah! sayeth the frog. *You're not sticking that thing up my Transom!*

I mouthed the word, looking at Grym.

"It's the backend of a boat," he told me. "He's an amphibian so he appears to believe that makes him nautical."

"Now who's on drama overload?" I said, snorting.

Stick that thermometer up your butt and we'll see who does drama, the frog exclaimed. *Cheh, Cheh, Cheh. Hachoo!*

"Yeah," I said, frowning. "You sound splendiferous."

I'm just going to take a little nap, He said. *It's fine. I'm fine. I'm...*

"Splendiferous. I know." I stood over Slimy as he tucked himself under the heat lamp and fell asleep. Or, I thought he was sleeping. It was hard to tell since he slept with his eyes open most of the time.

So creepy.

Grym came up beside me and dropped an arm around my shoulders, giving me a quick hug. "If he's not better in the morning, we'll take him to the vet."

Given the unique type of "pets" that I had, our vet was located at Enchanted City's one and only supernormal hospital. It wouldn't be a kindness to take Vel or Slimy to a human vet. They might stab the poor guy's psyche without meaning to by barking explosively or reciting the thesaurus.

I nodded, but a frown still sat on my face.

The dividing door opened and I swung my gaze toward the whirling dervish speeding my way. "Miss!" Hobs said. "You need to come look."

Before I could ask what was going on, he was gone again. The only evidence he'd even been there was the quivering of a picture under a wave of displaced air.

I took a deep breath and started after him, certain that whatever he wanted to show me wasn't good.

There was a small group clustered around the crack in the library.

Wicked sat close to Sebille, his tail whipping with agitation. He turned his orange gaze my way and hissed softly. I chose to believe he wasn't hissing at me, but rather at whatever he was observing as Baca moved a trowel of some kind over the bottom of the crack.

I narrowed my gaze on the break in the concrete. "Does that look wider to you?"

Grym nodded. "A little, yeah." He'd followed me in and joined the group. "Is that Quick Concrete?" he asked our resident brownie.

Baca didn't take her eyes off her work as she scooped up another glob of some grayish stuff in a small bucket and applied it to the crack. She nodded. "Magically enhanced Quick Concrete. I've added anti-decay to the mix hoping that might stop the spread."

Even as she explained what she was doing, something crackled near the spot where she worked and a big hunk of concrete broke off to coat the filler she was applying. She pressed the tool onto the spot, holding it there for a beat before trying once again to fill the crack.

An even bigger piece of the floor broke off as she worked.

Baca sat back on her heels with a sigh. "It's only making it worse."

"I guess that would have been too easy," I told the

brownie, patting her on her tiny shoulder. "Do you have any other ideas?"

Baca frowned. "We need to determine what is infecting the concrete."

I frowned. "Infecting it? You mean, like a disease?"

"Kind of. But not really. The artifact is not the crack itself, but the entity infecting it. I guess you could call it a magical infection."

"So, how do you heal a magical infection?" Grym asked.

"Medicine," Hobs said, nodding as if what he'd said was as clear as day.

I looked at Sebille. "Did your mom have any ideas?"

The sprite nodded. "One. But you aren't going to like it."

I expelled air. "What?"

"Moon moss."

I blinked. "Moss from the actual moon?"

Sebille nodded. "Yes. But hopefully we won't need to travel to the moon to collect it. Do you remember that asteroid that slammed into the Enchanted Forest last year?"

"Yeah," Grym said, nodding. "Does your mom think there's moon moss on that?"

"She thinks it's possible. But first we have to find it."

I grimaced. Finding anything in the Enchanted Forest was almost impossible. First, because the place was massive, tangled, and insidiously dangerous. And second, because magic in the forest doesn't act as expected. It doesn't sit still. And it doesn't follow the rules of nature. The asteroid could have landed at the base of the Enchanted Falls, the world's largest and most magical waterfall system, and it could be on the other side of the forest a week later.

"Okay. Well, that's worth pursuing," I said, sounding tired even to myself. "Knock, knock," Lea said just before she stuck her head through the door. "Hey. I came to treat your patient."

"Patient?" Sebille asked. "What patient?"

I started toward Lea. "Slimy's sick." I gave my best friend a smile. "I didn't hear the front door jangle."

"That's because the bell's cracked."

Rubbing my hands over my face, I said, "Of course it is." I slipped my arm through hers and we turned back to the bookstore and the hacking, sneezing squish. "Did I call you and forget I did it? I thought about asking you to come take a look at him, but got distracted."

"I was in here earlier and heard him coughing." She held up a small baggie and shook it. "I have wartwood dust."

"Will that cure him?"

"It should. Especially with the little somethin' somethin' I added." She winked, wiggling her fingers.

Giving her an impulsive hug, I squeezed her tight. "Thanks, girlfriend. I'm starting to freak out a little bit. The last thing I need is a sick frog."

"No luck with the cracks?" Her gaze lifted to the cracked bell on the door.

My gaze followed hers and I sighed. "Not yet. But I'm glad you stopped by because Baca thinks the problem is a magical infection. I wondered if you could assess it for a potential herbal cure?" If I got lucky, she'd have some other kind of herb that would work so we wouldn't have to go to the forest to forage for space moss.

"I'd be glad to look," she said. "But I can tell you without even looking that you're going to need Moon moss."

I wrinkled my nose. "Really?"

Lea nodded, setting her baggie on the table and reaching inside to pinch some of the herb between her fingers. "That's the best general cure for magical infections. I actually need to get Queen Sindra some for the fruit trees."

My brows peaked. "The cracking caused your fruit trees to fall?"

"It looks that way." Lea sprinkled the herb into Slimy's pool.

"Ah," I said. There went the hope of not going into the Enchanted Forest.

6

MUMMUMMEMUMAMUMCA

As much as I was dreading a visit to Queen Kaith of the trolls, I was even more reluctant to enter the Enchanted Forest in search of alien moss. I'd had too many bad experiences in the forest to embrace the idea of stepping foot in there again. Between killing wraiths, man-eating voids, deadly witches, woman-eating multi-headed snakes, and an endless array of other dangers, the forest was not only terrifying, it was actually dangerous to our health.

Despite all that, I was stuffing supplies into a backpack the next morning, wondering how many protein bars and bottles of water I could fit in there and still bring underwear and a change of clothing with me.

Since Croakies was closed, I was surprised to hear the fractured clang of the doorbell ringing through my small apartment. I stuck my head out of the door and yelled into the artifact library. "Sebille? Did you leave the front door unlocked?"

The soft buzz of approaching wings came from the nether regions of the library, where the sprite had made a home inside a magical shrinking box on a shelf. I didn't even really know where the box was hidden. She'd made it a point, a couple of years earlier, to clandestinely move into the library after being thrown out of her apartment above the vaping store across the street.

Something about over-vaping a customer with one of her own, private recipes, and then turning him into a slug.

Slimy business.

Sebille buzzed into view, her natural sprite form about the size of a large dragonfly but more colorful. "I did lock it. And I set the wards. Maybe it's your stone-faced boyfriend. Didn't you give him a key?"

I narrowed my gaze on her. "Why are you bad-mouthing Grym? He bought you donuts yesterday and Tacos last week."

Sebille buzzed in place in front of me. "Yeah. I actually got to lick the donut box after he and the hobgoblin ate them all. I only got to smell the tacos before they were gone."

"Grym didn't eat any of those donuts, and he and I had already had our tacos at the restaurant. If the food disappeared before you could get to it, that was Hobs and Baca. Don't blame Grym."

The sprite flung up a hand. "Whatever."

The dividing door creaked open and got stuck about midway on the cracked floor. A wide, flat, yellow face topped by orange hair and a matching short beard popped through the abbreviated opening. "Did you know you have a sick frog in here?"

Sebille and I shared a look.

"Yes. He's on medicine. Um. Who are you?"

The creature squeezed her massive yellow body through the opening, grunting and groaning as she did, and then brushed a meaty palm over the front of her shirt. Said article of clothing had a low vee-neck that highlighted a deep cleavage covered in curly orange chest hair. She'd tucked the shirt into camo-patterned cargo pants that stopped just below her knees. Her forearms and calves were also covered in dense orange hair. Several heavy bracelets, appearing to be made of rock, clunked together when she lifted her arm. "Didn't Rhorr tell you I was coming?"

Ah. Realization clicked. "The Rock Meister?"

She made a noisy flourish with her bracelet-bedecked arm and bowed. "Aelice the Amiable at your service."

"Aelice..."

"The Amiable," the Meister said. She enunciated slowly, as if she were teaching a toddler the language.

"Er, yes. Aelice the Amiable, did you by chance notice that the front door was locked when you came inside?"

"I did not notice that because it wasn't." She pointed at the dividing door. "Like this entry, that one has been greatly compromised."

My eyes went wide. "It's cracked too?"

"It is. Now, let's not waste any more time. Where is my project?"

"Your project?" Sebille snapped. "This isn't a game, Aelice..."

"The Amiable."

Sebille growled a little. "How about I just call you ATA? The other takes too long to say and we're short on time."

The Meister's lips quivered. "That's reasonable." She cocked her head. "The crack?" She nodded toward the obvious breach in the concrete across the room. She didn't really need us to show her where it was, but I appreciated that she didn't just march in and take over. One never knew what an ogre could do. Especially one that had been described more than once as "wily".

As we headed toward the widest part of the fissure, I noticed thin tendrils of it had spread toward the wall between the library and the bookstore. Would it eventually crack the wall too?

My stomach twisted with alarm. At the rate the toxic artifact was going, there would be nothing left of Croakies within the space of a month.

ATA dropped to her knees beside the crevice, which was nearly five feet across at its widest point and was already sending slender tendrils in several directions. I noted that one tendril was halfway to the stairs that led to my upstairs apartment.

"Please tell me you can stop this," I said, my voice tight with worry.

Aelice lifted a thick digit to silence me and then closed her eyes, inhaling deeply. The Meister held her breath for long enough that I started to worry she'd pass out, and when she finally expelled it, she blew it along the crack.

If anything happened, I didn't see it.

"What do you think?" I asked, earning another quelling digit from the ogre.

I fidgeted in silence—or what I could manage in the way of silence—as the Meister lowered her head and stuck her nose into the crevice. She inhaled again, stood up, and stepped over the breached concrete before dropping back to her knees and exhaling onto the artifact.

The second time, I saw a tiny orange spark of magic.

I opened my mouth to ask her what that meant, but she turned a gimlet glare on me and my lips snapped shut.

Aelice pushed to her feet and reached into one of the oversized pockets of her cargo pants, pulling out a handful of what I guessed was probably rock dust. She closed her eyes and began to chant, the words indecipherable. It sounded something like "Mummummemumamumca."

Then she threw the dust into the crevice.

Flame flared from the crack and rose above Aelice's six-feet-six form, burning out within seconds.

"What did that mean?"

The Meister's lips curled and she growled at me.

I took a big step back, lifting my hands in a defensive posture.

Aelice frowned, but the expression didn't seem to be directed at me.

Chewing my bottom lip, I waited for her to give me her findings.

To my surprise and alarm, she dropped to her knees again and bent over the crack. Her long, purple tongue snaked out and swiped the inside of the fissure.

I grimaced.

Aelice sighed. "It is as I feared."

My stomach twisted with panic. "What?"

She turned a hostile, narrowed gaze on me. "Is this your doing?"

I flinched, pointing stupidly at my own chest. "Me? No. Of course not. Why would I crack my own shop?"

Aelice kept her assessing gaze locked onto me. "Do you have a hobgoblin?"

I tensed, suspecting that I knew what she was going to say. The temptation to lie and say no was nearly overwhelming. I opened my mouth to do just that, but the sprite cracked her poisonous maw first. "Yes. Did he do this?"

I deflated, dreading the outcome if he had. I didn't know if I could actually fling Hobs into the streets to fend for himself. My logical side told me it would be good for him to learn to take care of himself. But my emotional side was weeping all over that nasty logic and calling it names.

"Unlikely," the Meister said. "But hobgoblins have access to other dimensions. He can get me what I need."

I perked up at her words, fighting a childish urge to poke my tongue out at Sebille. "What do you need?"

"Filigreed rock from the center of the earth. Or near enough to the center. It doesn't actually thrive with that much heat." The explanation didn't seem to be directed toward me. She was muttering.

"Um," I said. "Ah, er..."

"Nicely put, Naida," the sprite snarked. "I couldn't have said it better myself."

I glowered at her. "Will Hobs know what filigreed rock is?" I asked doubtfully.

ATA shrugged. "Any hobgoblin worth his salt has hunted for unique rocks. Where do you think diamonds first came from? And lava rock?"

"Because everybody wants lava rock for their flower beds," Sebille said helpfully.

I threw her another glare. Irritated that she was being snarky rather than helpful.

ATA nodded in agreement, clueless that she was being mocked.

"Precisely." The Meister reached both hands into over-sized pockets on her thighs and extracted something green. It looked like moss. "Send the hobgoblin to me so I can give him his marching orders."

"Um," I responded, unsure if I wanted to send Hobs to the center or the earth.

"Sparkling conversation," the sprite said. "I'm tongue-tied by your brilliance."

I widened my eyes in warning and slashed a finger across my throat. "I'll see if he's busy."

ATA was packing the moss into the crack. She stopped at my vague statement and slowly turned my way, staring at me with such disgust that I found myself promising to deliver Hobs without delay.

She inclined her head and went back to work. As I turned toward his den location to fetch Hobs she stopped me. "Keeper?"

I turned back. "Yes?"

She offered me a scroll. I blinked. It hadn't been in her hand an instant earlier. Had she pulled it from one of the oversized pockets?

Guessing what it was, I shoved my hands into my pockets so I wouldn't accidentally grab it. "What's that?"

"It's an accord. You'll need to sign this if you want me to work for you. It says I'll be staying in that apartment upstairs while I'm here, and will require three meals a day, all hot, and a snack before bed."

"Um," I said, much to Sebille's delight. I ignored her snort and said. "That's my..."

"That is all," the Meister said, dismissing me. "You're holding up my progress." She shoved the scroll into my middle, nearly relocating my liver to my spine.

"We certainly wouldn't want to do that," I gasped as I spun on my heel and stalked away. I shoved the scroll into the first trash can I encountered. The Meister was being wily and I wouldn't be signing the agreement. The king himself warned me against making any agreements with her. She was presumably there at the king's command. She couldn't refuse to help.

Could she?

Shaking off my doubts, I squared my shoulders. It would

be inconvenient if the ogre took over my apartment for a few days. But the inconvenience would be worth it if King Rhorr's expert could save Croakies. Still, I had to bite back several harsh words that I wanted to say to the odious woman. "Rick and Maxine are so pleasant," I muttered to myself.

I sighed as I headed for the hole in the wall between two of the library's enormous artifact shelves where Hobs had made his home. I never thought I'd look forward to a couple of days in the Enchanted Forest.

What a difference an hour could make.

7

TECHNICALLY, IT'S THE
MOHOROVICIC DISCONTINUITY

Hobs lifted his chin and tried to look brave as he stared up, up, and up at the enormous ogre. Only someone who knew him as well as I did would notice the slight tremor in the tuft of hair between his ears that indicated fear.

I stood close to the tiny hobgoblin, my stern expression warning Aelice not to abuse the little guy. Hobs reached up and threaded his long fingers through mine. His felt unusually warm.

"All you need to do is separate the weave between this plane and the core dimension and find me some of this..." Aelice lifted her enormous hands and wiggled her sausage fingers. The air in front of her shimmered and thickened, colored motes swirling and spinning until a discernible picture formed.

Discernible...but not one I recognized. It was a shadowy place, the edges of the vision showing layers of veiny rock. Off to the side, I could see a large filigreed formation. The strange structure rose from the ground in misshapen but artful loops and swirls. It looked delicate, though something told me it was far from it. "Where is this?" I asked, taking a step closer and squinting at the vision hanging in the air.

"The lithosphere," Aelice said distractedly. "Technically, it's the Mohorovicic Discontinuity, but you don't need that much detail. Suffice it to say this location is about 30 miles below the surface." Her gaze was locked on Hobs, who'd moved closer to the vision and had extended a finger to try to touch the lacy rock at the base. "Pretty."

Aelice blew a raspberry. "This has nothing to do with aesthetics, boy. There's no stronger binder in the universe. That rock is going to fix your crack problem."

I liked the sound of that, but not the way she spoke to Hobs, so I renewed my glare.

Not that Aelice seemed to notice. "Well? What are you waiting for, boy? Get hoppin'."

When Hob's tuft went from a quiver to a quake, I squeezed his sweaty hand. "Aelice..."

"The Amiable," she added with a single, cocked eyebrow.

"ATA," I corrected, unwilling to allow the creature anywhere near the word "amiable". "What exactly are you hoping to get from this lacy rock?"

The ogre rolled her eyes, which were a pinpoint of orange in a sea of white, and crossed her beefy arms over her massive chest. "I've already explained, but I'll do it again. Why the king didn't tell me you were a simpleton, I do not know."

I might have growled. Just a little. "Humor me."

She sighed. "Filigreed rock is a strong base. It's like steel netting that allows rock to rebuild and enhances its strength."

That sounded promising. "So, you think..."

"Know. I know."

"You know that this filigreed rock will allow the cracked concrete to rebuild?"

"Yes."

Sebille frowned. "What about everything else?"

We scanned a look at the cracked wall. To my horror, the crack in the drywall appeared to have widened in the half-hour since I'd last looked at it.

The Rock Meister punched her shoulders toward her ears, seeming unconcerned. "I'm a Rock Meister, keeper. I'm not a Wood Meister or a Wall Meister. The king commanded me to fix the crack in your concrete. That's all I'm going to do."

Disappointment filled me. It wasn't perfect. But it was better than nothing. Since the breach had begun in the concrete floor, maybe it would stop if we defeated it there. Then we could just repair or replace the other surfaces where damage occurred. "Okay. We'd appreciate anything you can do to help."

"Dang straight," the Meister grumbled.

Sebille's hands formed into fists and sparks flared in her iridescent green gaze.

I cleared my throat and the sprite glowered at me.

Shaking my head, I forced a smile. Turning to Hobs, I asked, "Do you think Baca can help you mine some of that filigreed rock?"

His eyes lit with pleasure. Aside from the fact that he and Baca were very close, the little brownie was very handy with projects of the type we were asking him to pursue. "Yes, Miss. She'd be very helpful."

"Good." My smile relaxed and felt more natural in the face of his relieved pleasure. "Can you see if she wants to go?"

He shot away in a blur of white and I turned to The Meister. "ATA, just a bit of advice. When it comes to hobgoblins and brownies, you literally get better results with honey than vinegar."

The ogre snorted, something gross flying out of her wide nose and then getting sucked back in when she sniffed. "Do I act like I carry vinegar around with me?"

"You act like you subsist on little else," Sebille mumbled.

I fought a grin. She wasn't wrong. "Okay. We need to prepare for a foray into the Forest," I told the ogre. "Wish us well."

The Meister snorted again. Sebille and I took a large step back. Just in case. "Why would I do that? Your forays are none of my concern."

"Right." I met Sebille's wide-eyed stare. "Go time in twenty," I told my goggle-eyed assistant.

"I'm actually looking forward to it," she responded.

"Yeah," I agreed. "Me too."

THE ENCHANTED FOREST was still and quiet.

Unnaturally quiet.

I tugged on the straps of my backpack and glanced around at our little group, noting that we'd all scrunched closer to each other, moving through the unpredictable forest as if we were already under siege.

We probably were and didn't know it yet.

A long, hoarse shriek stabbed the air in the near distance and I jumped, giving a decidedly girlish shriek of my own.

Bodies pressed closer to me on both sides as Lea gave in

to the urge for security in numbers and Grym gave in to his desire to protect.

I glanced around, looking for my friend, Rustin, and found him on his knees on the ground, lowering his top half to sniff the dirt of the path we'd been following. A tall, well-made man of thirty-something, Rustin had a piercing blue gaze covered by a pair of wire-rimmed spectacles sitting on his classically perfect nose. His thick mane of black hair hung in his eyes as he sniffed the ground.

"What are you doing?" I asked, frowning at him.

Rustin ignored my question, his brows lowering as he sniffed again.

I shared a look with Grym. He only shrugged, his expression seeming to declare that nobody understood shifters.

Expelling a breath, I nodded. I couldn't disagree. Rustin might have come to his dual nature late in life, when his abhorrent family, not including Madeline or Maude Quilleran, had put his soul into a frog...Mr. Slimy...and he'd ended up with no body. After many months of research and work, Maddie and Maude had managed to give Rustin back not one, but two physical forms. His human form was every bit as pleasing as it had been before he was extricated from it. But his magical form was...phenomenal.

Another shriek stabbed the air.

I jumped, my heart pounding against my ribs.

"What was that?" I breathed out, my face hot with embarrassment for overreacting.

A nearby buzzing sound drew our gazes upward, to the sprite who hovered overhead. She'd turned buggy and tucked herself beneath the protective arms of a Locuss tree.

Apparently, I wasn't the only one who was overreacting.

A magical cousin to the locust tree, the Locuss had long

skinny leaves that were forked on the ends like a snake's tongue. The tree's pretty purple-black flowers were rumored to emit a poisonous mist if you sniffed them, but I had no intention of finding out if it was true.

Sebille crossed her skinny arms over her flat chest and sniffed. She looked less than fairy-like with her green and orange scarf around her neck and the bright purple and yellow striped leggings clinging to her bony legs. The pink in her cheeks added an embarrassed tint to her own personal color wheel. "I was just trying to see if the trouble was in this tree."

"Uh huh," I murmured, a grin trying to curve onto my face. "Did you find the dastardly villain snuffling the poisonous flowers?"

She sniffed again and buzzed off, head high and posture stiff. The sprite didn't like to be caught with her dignity flapping around her ankles. Which was odd, given the way she generally dressed.

I turned to Grym. "I'm going to assume that was just some random critter who got startled by our passage."

"You know what they say about assuming, right?"

I narrowed my eyes at him. "Lea, do you have any idea which way we need to go?"

She pulled a metal contraption from her pocket and held it out in front of her. Two slender needles spun and rocked beneath some kind of magic before finally settling. My bestie frowned at the compass, whose needles pointed in opposite directions. She glanced to her right and then to her left. "The forest's diverse equivalence is confusing my compass."

I wasn't surprised. The phrase alone was confusing me. But I nodded. "Can we split the difference and spread out? Maybe we'll stumble across it that way."

She sighed. "I guess that's the best we can do. But we still have two directions we'll need to go. The needles are pointing directly opposite each other. I'd been hoping it would give us a geographic slice that we could easily cover. There's no telling where the moss is given this range."

"Wouldn't it be at either of the two points?" Grym asked reasonably.

"That would be too easy," Lea told him with a wry smile. "This compass doesn't point directly at anything. It projects an area to search."

"What a stupid compass," Sebille said.

We all glanced up to find her striding toward us in her human form. She'd pulled the scarf tighter around her skinny neck as if she were cold.

"Where'd you get the compass?" she asked Lea.

Lea grinned. "Off your shelves."

Sebille frowned, scanning me a look.

"It's an artifact," I told the sprite. "A really old one. I found it when I was dusting the back shelves last week. It's actually perfect for what we need." I grimaced. "Theoretically." The magical compass's current orientation was less than helpful, but the paperwork with the artifact had described it as a tracking compass. I glanced at Lea. "Try it again, Lea. Maybe the energy of the forest has settled by now."

Three more tries didn't get us much better results. On the last attempt, we managed to carve about four degrees off our search area and decided to go with that. At least we could focus our search on the East side of our current position, rather than having to search both the East and West.

We set off within the determined parameters of the compass, our path outlined by a shimmering golden light that bathed the ground at our feet. High above our heads, the sun toasted us in waves of heat that hadn't existed when we'd left Croakies.

In the heart of Enchanted City, the skies had been a leaden gray. The temps had been in the sixties, with a drizzle that, in addition to the scent of ozone, promised it would only degrade from there. I fully expected to return home to find rain pelting the streets and structures, and running like a river through the ever-growing crack bisecting Croakies.

I sighed.

The sound must have hinted at my despair because Grym bumped me with his shoulder. "You okay?"

I wasn't okay. I'd always felt a bit inadequate in my position as KoA. A keeper of magical artifacts holds a lot of power and carries a lot of responsibility on her shoulders. When I'd accepted the job, I'd known I wasn't good enough to do it well. I hadn't even known about magic until shortly before I'd become the intern to the current keeper.

I was the poster girl for the concept of trial by fire.

But despite that questionable beginning, I had managed to gain a measure of competence at my job. It helped that I was surrounded by truly talented magical beings. Still, I was battling a strong sense of being out of my depth with the current challenge. Granted, I wasn't the only one who had no clue how to defeat the toxic magic. But knowing the PTB were also out of their depth with the current problem didn't make me feel better. If they couldn't help me, I was truly on my own.

"Naida?"

I forced a smile and bumped him back with my shoulder. "I'm fine. I'm just thinking."

He opened his mouth to respond, his dark-caramel gaze holding mine.

A blood-chilling roar tore the otherwise silent day, followed by the sound of something big thundering in our direction.

At first glance, I thought it was a bear. A big bear. Its paws slammed into the earth as it loped in our direction, the leaves of the Locuss tree trembling under their impact.

"Get behind a tree!" Grym bellowed, grabbing my arm and pushing me firmly toward the Locuss as his muscular body flexed and swelled into the change to his gargoyle.

Too quickly, the massive black creature burst through a thicket of underbrush and roared again. The creature's round black eyes rolled skyward until all I could see were the whites. Though it had the shape of a bear, two of its fangs curved down toward its chin, like something from the dinosaur age, and its hair was pale brown, the thick pelt set in whorls all over its tall form. The creature's snout was moist and brown, the nostrils flaring and shrinking as if it was scenting the air.

Stumbling backward toward the thickest tree trunk I could find, I kept my attention focused on the charging creature. A sour stench wafted off its whorl-decorated frame. A scent that was too much like fear for my comfort. A terrified animal was dangerous.

But what does the boogie man fear?

As the bear burst into the area where we stood, it opened its quivering maw and roared again. Spotting Grym in the middle of the path, the creature skidded to a halt and rose to its back legs, bellowing so loudly I dropped to my knees and covered my ears.

Grym rushed forward and slammed into it, wrapping his huge, impermeable frame around the creature in a bear hug. But, as strong as he was, the bear likely outweighed him by a lot. It reared back and slammed a massive paw into Grym's chest, sending him flying along the well-worn path.

"Ah!" Lea exclaimed behind me.

"Um, Naida?" Sebille said, her tone a tight warning.

Hot air bathed the back of my neck.

And I went very still.

8

DOES A CATERPILLAR HAVE TOO MANY KNEES?

A loud chuffing sound twisted my nerves into knots. I went rigid with fear. Hot breath bathed my neck and blew tendrils of hair into my face, where globules of monster spit made it stick. The creature's breath smelled like barbeque and smoke wafted over me with every breath.

I frowned.

A scuffing step preceded the feeling of soft fur tickling my exposed flesh. Nostrils snuffled against my skin just above the neckline of my tee-shirt, leaving behind a moist trail. A low growl followed, as if the creature didn't like the way I smelled.

I fought the desire to shudder as the moist touch tickled my sensitive skin.

A feral scent rolled over me, a breeze carrying the monster's wild perfume into my space.

"Naida, don't move," Grym said, his voice soft and wary. He'd stopped fighting the bear thing as soon as our new adversary appeared, and I pictured them both staring at the monster behind me.

I was dying to answer...bad pun...sorry. But I couldn't make myself speak. Something told me I'd regret the words. One way or another.

Another roar disturbed the fraught silence and the snuffling stopped, the heated breath sliding away as the thing turned its head. *Yes.* I thought. *That's the bad guy. I'm the good guy. Go over there.*

The creature at my back roared in response and I jumped with a cry, immediately ducking my head as if that would save me. The monster leaped into motion, its golden-furred shoulder knocking me sideways as it met the bear-thing's challenge.

I hit the ground hard, the pain reverberating from my sacroiliac all the way up my spine. "Ouch!" Dust puffed up around me and I coughed, then coughed again and sneezed hard enough to twinge my aching muscles, causing me to cry out again in pain.

Grym dropped to his knees beside me, yanking me into a hug. He held me so tight I couldn't breathe. "Thank the goddess!" Grym murmured into my hair. "I thought he was going to lose his mind there for a minute." I was happy to see that my gargoyle had donned his clothes again before returning to me.

"He really needs to work on that," I said, giving in to a shiver at the remembered feeling of having an ancient supernormal thinking about having me for an afternoon snack.

In the distance, the bear thing and Rustin in his Chimera form battled for dominance, the sounds savage and terrifying. I ground down on the urge to take off running and not stop until I reached Grym's boxy gray SUV and locked myself inside.

Lea came out of her hiding spot, her face pale as she

dropped down beside me. "I don't think I'm ever going to get used to that," she said, rubbing my back as her gaze strayed toward the sounds in the near distance. After a moment, she seemed to shake it off and she turned back to me. "Are you hurt?"

"Does emotionally traumatized count?"

"It does for me," Lea said.

"We need to keep moving," Sebille said.

I looked up into her bright green gaze and noted that her freckles stood out more than usual. Her face was paper white, and there was a slight tremor in her hands. I knew how she felt. Every time I witnessed Rustin in his monstrous form, feeling the pure savagery of his second nature and knowing that it held my fragile life in its massive paws, it was like dying for a few seconds and coming back with a new appreciation for life.

A pain-filled yelp signaled the end of the fight. One of the two combatants would soon return, and I wasn't sure which of them would be worse.

Apparently agreeing with me, Grym helped me to my feet and tugged me toward the trees.

"I can cast a barrier spell around us," Sebille said, her voice husky with concern.

"I'll strengthen whatever you come up with," Lea said.

A moment later, as we huddled behind two large Locuss trees staring in the direction Rustin had gone, I was half relieved and half concerned when our friend stepped out of the dense underbrush and stood before us.

The thing was enormous.

Though I was a respectable five feet nine inches tall, the Chimera—I had trouble thinking of it as Rustin because it was so inhuman and terrifying—was nearly twice as tall as I was. Its wings were massive. They'd have to be to carry the enormous creature through the air. Its nostrils flared and a hollow chuff sounded, the thick golden mane quivering with interest. The creature's eyes were golden too. They were intelligent eyes, but not in any way human.

I swallowed hard as the Chimera's feral gaze fell on me. It lifted its leathery dragon wings, which had curved claws at the apex of their bony frames, and shuffled its scaled back legs, bringing attention to the deadly-looking claws, which could rip a human apart in a single slash.

Its tail, thicker than a lion's but with the same general shape, the Chimera had a ball of fur on the end like the big cat's. Part dragon and part lion, the creature carried the fierceness of both species in its strong lines and confident presence.

When it continued to eye me, I wiggled my fingers in a wave and gave it what was probably a terrified smile. "Hey, Rustin. Did you get the bad guy?"

The Chimera shimmied, twitched, and disappeared in a puff of painfully white light, leaving behind Rustin, looking chagrined, but thankfully fully dressed. He hurried toward me. "Naida, are you okay? I'm so sorry I sniffed you."

I couldn't help it, I laughed. It was a slightly maniacal-sounding laugh, but it was the best I could do under the circumstances. "It's fine. You didn't eat me so that's good."

He stopped several feet away and fixed me with an apologetic gaze. "I don't know what happened. One minute I was me and the next I was...him." Rustin grimaced.

I widened my eyes in surprise. It was the first time he'd admitted to feeling separate from his Chimera form.

Reaching out, I clasped his hand. "You were a perfect gentleman. Don't worry."

Sebille snorted. "A gentleman with a furry butt."

Rustin narrowed his gaze on her. "And what were you doing noticing my butt?"

"It was kind of hard to miss. The thing's huge. And that tail...Rapunzel could clamber up that thing to escape an over-zealous Prince Charming."

"I think you're mixing fairytales, Sebille," Lea said, grinning.

"Fairy tails?" Sebille snorted. "Good one, Lea."

My bestie rolled her eyes.

"We should keep moving," Grym said, his gaze sliding skyward. "It's going to be dark soon. I'd really like to be out of here before night falls. Does everybody agree?"

"Does a caterpillar have too many knees?" Sebille asked.

Grym frowned, probably not sure if the question was rhetorical. Finally, he said, "Uh, they probably have just the right number."

"That was a joke," Sebille said, shaking her head. She rubbed her arms as she glanced around. The shadows were already bleeding from the heavy vegetation surrounding us.

"I definitely agree," I said, nodding enthusiastically. "The sooner the better."

Lea glanced down at the compass again and her eyes lit up. "Our search area has tightened."

"Praise the goddess," I said, sighing with relief. "Things are looking up."

~

IT DIDN'T TAKE LONG before things started looking down again.

We stopped for a brief rest an hour later, our gazes sliding toward the encroaching darkness as we sipped water and munched protein bars. For the better part of the time we'd been walking, something had been stalking us from the air. Something big and dark. I'd nearly caught a glimpse of it a few times, but somehow it had managed to blend into the growing darkness and escape identification.

Only the muscular pulse of its wings warned that it was there. I would have liked to believe that, whatever it was, it wasn't antagonistic toward the small group of magic users in its woods. But an icy antagonism seemed to waft downward whenever it flew past overhead. And the dire atmosphere it left behind was all I needed to make my strides quicken and keep my head on a swivel looking for trouble.

"We should keep moving," Grym said, his voice soft and his tone wary. Like mine, his gaze slid skyward, trying to see through the dense, overarching tree line to the potential foe above.

A bellowing hiss stabbed into my nerves and I sucked in a startled gasp. I glanced at Sebille. "Do you recognize that call?"

She shook her head. "It sounds like one of the dinosaurs we encountered when we took the time-travelling tortoise to the Jurassic era."

Lea nodded, "Good times."

My throat closed up with dread. That was exactly what I'd thought too. "Is it possible Tildy returned to that age and dragged a dinosaur back with her?" I felt silly asking the question, but under the circumstances, I thought it needed to be asked.

"Unlikely?" Sebille said.

I narrowed my gaze on her. "Was that an opinion? Or a question?"

"Both?"

I expelled air. "Let's pick up the pace. Maybe whatever it

is will go away. It hasn't attacked us yet. So, maybe it doesn't want to."

Sebille snorted. She'd always gotten a kick out of my attempts at positive thinking. For her part, she preferred negative thoughts. That way, she liked to tell me, if things went south, she wasn't disappointed.

"It doesn't seem aggressive," Lea said, "Just curious." I lifted my fist and we bumped knuckles. Lea was a Polly Positive too. It was probably the reason we got along so well.

Another bellowing hiss brought my hackles up and I took a couple of running steps before realizing such an escalation might engage the creature's prey drive. But then several more hisses joined the first, and the thrum of wings grew louder.

There was more than one!

By the time the tree limbs above us started to shudder under the movement of way too many oversized antagonists, I was running whether it made any sense or not. My fight-or-flight instincts got the best of me and I was off.

Or maybe it was the firm shove between my shoulder blades and Grym's shouted growl to "Run!" that set me off.

Either way, the movement did exactly what I'd been afraid it would.

With a collective bellow of breathy sound, our stalkers shot from the trees, and set off after us on a mingled roar.

9

IRENE, IRENE, IRENE!

"I hate this goddess-be-danged forest," I yelled. My statement was wheezy and tight, fear having gotten a firm grip on my seizing lungs. Behind me, Grym used his strength and size to batter away the massive birds that were diving and striking at us with sharply curved beaks.

I'd already been stabbed in the back and arms several times, and clawed with sharp black talons a few more. Blood dripped off my flailing fists and ran down my back beneath my shirt.

Even as they flew and dove, the birds' horrifying roar made me stumble every time I heard it. It really did sound like a dinosaur.

Something that felt like a bullet slammed into my skull, making me cry out and nearly fall to my knees. Grym got a hand on my arm and kept me upright, then gave me a gentle push to keep me moving.

Though I didn't dare look over my shoulder at the creatures chasing us, I'd seen enough to get the impression of black and gray bodies that were about three feet long with ruffs of spiky golden feathers behind pale-colored heads. The birds had fierce red eyes and oversized, bulbous beaks that struck bone with the force of a hammer. They seemed oddly familiar, but my mind was too adrenaline-saturated to release the memory.

Grym grunted and gasped. I started to turn, afraid he'd been hurt.

Before I could catch a glimpse of him, one of the birds slammed into me, striking me with the force of an animal much larger than it was. I hit the ground hard enough to knock the air from my lungs and skidded on my belly until I slammed into an aggressive tangle of oversized roots at the base of a tree. I wheezed out a breath as pain robbed me of any remaining air. Before I had time to shove to my feet again, they were on me, too many of them to fight. I was covered in large, feathered bodies, their massive talons digging for purchase on my back and arms.

I screamed...or at least tried to. Between my raging terror and the moldy leaves and dust rising in a cloud from the torn earth around me, I was lucky to draw a breath. A bony projectile...a beak I presumed...thudded into my back and for a beat I thought my heart had stopped from the impact. If I'd been able to draw a good breath up until that point, it would have been the last one I took for a while.

A wheezing gasp filled my mouth and lungs with dust and I tried to cough but couldn't. There were no less than five of the things on top of me and it was getting difficult to know which would kill me first, their feral ravaging of my flesh or suffocation.

Screams and squawks sounded around me. I barely noticed, given that I was fighting for my life. But I had a moment to wonder why Rustin hadn't gone furry and fangy and eaten a few bad-tempered birds for dinner.

Surely they tasted like chicken.

Desperate and terrified, I fumbled in my pocket for something I could fight them off with. I pulled out a well-used tissue, a battered old penny I'd found on the street and kept with the hopes that it would be lucky (so much for that), and a candy wrapper.

Another, bigger bird joined the Naida buffet, its weight shoving me more deeply into the dust. The bigger bird's arrival was the proverbial straw on the camel's back. I lost my composure. Letting loose an enraged scream, I started kicking and punching. The violence of my reaction seemed to catch my unwelcome feather blanket by surprise. For a beat, they backed off, wings flapping as they hopped away from my fists and boots.

Unfortunately, it didn't take long for them to recover. They were likely irritated by the newest monster's arrival. It was massive and seemed to think I looked tasty. As it dove at me, its bulbous beak opened on one of those terrifying hissing roars, the others seemed to take offense. One in particular, slightly smaller than the others and covered in muddy brown feathers rather than the deep black most of them sported, lifted its wings and barreled toward the much bigger bird, beady red eyes glittering with affront.

To my surprise, the bigger bird backed off for a beat, eyeing the female who'd dared attack it. I would have laughed at the look of perplexity on its face if I didn't feel like ground hamburger.

Taking advantage of the female's interference, I scrambled away from the other birds, who all seemed to have joined forces in attacking Mr. Big.

My scrabbling fingers encountered a palm-sized flat rock

with sharp edges. It wasn't much of a weapon under the circumstances, but it was better than the used tissue.

I crouched under the tree I'd been thrown into with the rock clutched in my hand, looking around in an attempt to find my friends.

The place was a killing field.

As I took in all the broken bird corpses with glazed and cloudy eyes, dread made it hard to breathe. There were a lot of birds down, but there were also a lot left. Their squawks and roars accompanied the constant churning of branches high above my head. That was the moment I realized I was perched underneath what looked like a dozen more of the creatures. I gulped as a sea of beady red eyes focused down on me.

Grym was still on his feet, fists flying. He was covered in blood and surrounded by dead bird bodies. Where was everybody else? Had they been killed and carried off to be eaten?

Were they up in the trees, being tenderized over a knobby branch?

Tears burned my eyes. I couldn't think of that. We had to rid ourselves of the flying menace before I hung my emotions out for a good airing.

But...had they run off and left Grym and me to deal with the birds ourselves?

"Surely not," I murmured before I could stop myself. As soon as I said it, I grimaced. *Bee's buttocks.* What had I done?

The air sparkled in front of me and I leaned away from it, preparing myself as best I could for the dressing down I was about to receive. A burst of light made me blink and a tiny form suddenly hung in the air a foot away from my face, brown moth-like wings undulating like airborne manta rays.

A tiny, puckish face frowned in my direction. I gave the

pixie a little finger wave. Then doubled down on my mistake before I could stop myself. "Hey, Shirley."

Face as red as a tomato, the pixie placed her tiny hands on her teeny hips and glared at me. The muscles in her jaw flexed as she ground her coffee-stained teeth. "How many times have I told you not to call me that?" Shirley the pixie, otherwise known as the Witch-a-pedia of the magical world, was decidedly cranky about being called by her Earthly name.

I opened my mouth to apologize, but she attacked first.

"Shall I call you Naidaline?"

I grimaced.

"Or, if you'd prefer, I can call you by your middle name." Tiny brown brows slashed meanly and the pixie's round eyes glinted with anger. "Irene? How do you like that?"

I folded in on myself. I hadn't used my middle name since I was five and discovered my parents had named me after a grandmother who'd gone through life asking people to call her Janet because she'd hated the name so much.

"Irene, Irene, Irene," Shirley sang.

I scooted backward until I hit the rough bark of the tree, pain arcing through me as it abraded my torn flesh. "I'm..."

"Shall we try it on for size? Hmm?" the pixie buzzed higher, almost disappearing into the tree as she called into the suspiciously quiet night. "Naidaline Irene Griffith. How are you? You're looking a little pale, Naidaline. Would you rather I call you Irene? Irene, Irene, I..."

A broad, curved beak shot out from between the branches and snarfed up the pixie.

I blinked, not believing I'd seen what I'd seen. "Um." I frowned. "Ah, Shir...pixie?"

The vulture retreated and, a moment later, there was a clatter of wings and bellowed hisses as the massive committee of vultures became a kettle when they took to the air and flew away.

Banshee bunions! I was going to have to report to Maddie that we needed to recruit a new Witch-a-pedia for the magical world.

Hopefully she wouldn't think I'd murdered the nasty little creature to keep the world's worst name a secret forevermore.

Though it might be a justifiable offense. A jury of my peers would likely exonerate me. But there was always the danger that my mom or my brother might talk. I might have to threaten them too. *Hot yoga in the Sahara!* Escalation.

A distant hacking sound brought my head around just in time to see a large female hork up a thoroughly outraged if slightly slimy Shirley. The pixie appeared to still be alive. And feisty. She hovered in the air shaking a tiny fist at the vulture. The creature gave her a final bellowing hiss and took off after its friends.

I tried not to be disappointed as Shirley gave me the "I'm watching you" sign and popped away.

"Naida?"

"Huh?" I looked up at Lea. Please goddess she hadn't heard my full name. "Where were you guys?" I whined. "I thought you'd left us."

Lea gave me a weary smile. "Fighting these goddess-be-danged birds. The others are over there."

I shook my head, suddenly too sore and cranky to speak.

"Girl...you're a mess." Lea gently pulled my tee shirt up to look at my back. "Let me put some ointment on these wounds for you."

I nodded and followed her toward the group. They were taking stock of injuries and talking about the bird attack.

"...never seen the critters here so riled up," Rustin was

saying. "The forest has always had its dangers, but we've encountered two attacks in only a couple of hours. Something's going on."

"Don't you realize what those were?" Sebille asked him. She put her hands on her hips and gave Rustin a look that was both smug and irritated. A feat only Sebille could accomplish.

He narrowed his eyes on her. "Of course I do. I've spent enough time with them. My Chimera has even flown around the forest with them a few times."

"Speaking of your other form..." Grym said, lifting his brows in question. "Where was it? We could have used some help with those vultures."

"I was giving you help," Rustin objected angrily. "Didn't you see me throwing spells?"

"I was too busy being turned into bird buffet," Grym responded just as angrily.

I held up my hands. "Deep breaths guys. We're all on edge here. It's to be expected. But we need to stick together."

Lea nodded. "I agree with Naida. If we're going to navigate this forest and get that moss, we're going to have to work together."

Three combatants turned to her, scowling.

She flung up her hands and took a step back. "I'm on your side, remember?"

Grym came to his senses first. He closed his eyes and took deep breaths, then opened them and shook his head. "Sorry guys," he said. "And ladies." He grimaced. "I don't know what's wrong with me."

I nodded. "It's okay. We're all a little hot." We weren't the only ones. Shirley the pixie had been meaner than a pregnant snake in Hades with an ice cream craving. And the vultures. I swung my gaze around the group. "Those were Maddie's guard vultures, weren't they?"

Lea and Sebille nodded. Sebille's expression was still cranky. But since she was generally crabby, it didn't mean anything. "Why would Maddie's bird army attack us?"

"There's no reason," Rustin said. "Something is very wrong in the forest."

I really hoped it wasn't another one of the missing toxic artifacts. Our town wasn't big enough for two of them.

"More importantly," Lea said, "Why are they even in the forest? We're not close to Maddie's house, are we?"

We all glanced around, looking for landmarks that might tell us where we were. The problem with the Enchanted Forest...well, one of the many problems with it... was that it was saturated with magic. Old magic. Sometimes twisted magic. And one of its key features was the inability to lock onto any one location in the place. Things had a way of moving around in the forest. Which was one of the main reasons Maddie made her home there. As PTB for the Earthly dimension, Maddie was in singular danger from evil supernormals looking to steal power and influence.

"I don't know," I finally said. "This isn't a part of the forest that I've been to before." I didn't think. "I don't remember the Locuss tree grove. Do any of you?"

Grym shook his head. "I've never seen it before."

"Which doesn't really tell us anything since Madeline's house could have moved to a nearby spot five minutes ago."

A collective sigh filled the darkened air between us. Like Maddie's magical house changing on a whim, the magical forest had dropped full night on us in the space of time it took us to fight off the vultures.

"Why aren't the vultures protecting Maddie?" Lea asked.

Her hair looked blonde under the silver light of a full moon. That observation made me wonder if there were any were-wolves in the forest. Our recent string of bad luck made me expect there would be.

I snapped out of my thoughts when I heard Sebille say my name. "What? I'm sorry, I was thinking about the full moon."

All eyes slid skyward, and Lea's shoulders drooped. "Just peachy," she murmured. She'd evidently come to the same conclusion I had.

"I was asking who you spoke to when you called Madeline."

"Oh." I frowned thoughtfully. "Felonious was holding down the fort while Maddie and Maude were helping the Universal Council deal with the other rogue artifacts."

"Doesn't she generally take the guards with her when she goes to see the council?" Grym asked.

Rustin shook his head. "She doesn't. But she'd have left them with instructions to stick close to home. Even when she's not there, she has to worry about protecting confidential documents and her position as a Power."

"Then why are they rampaging through the forest?" I asked, repeating Lea's previous question.

"Vultures love Locuss flowers," Sebille said.

"But they wouldn't have disobeyed Maddie's orders," Rustin insisted.

"Which brings us back to Naida's question," Grym said, radiating concern. "What made the vulture guard leave Maddie's home, and pick a fight in the Enchanted Forest?"

What indeed, I asked myself. Hoping their presence in the forest didn't mean additional bad news for the absent PTB. "What if the crack at Croakies is affecting more than just physical structures," I asked. "What if it's cracking minds too?"

I hated the look that question put on my friends' faces. But it had to be asked.

Because if that was happening, our timeline for stopping the toxic artifact had just gotten tighter.

10

DAFT YE BE, MY BARNACLED FOE

The moon was high in the sky, threaded with pale, wispy clouds by the time we found the moss. If it hadn't been for Lea being there, I was pretty sure we'd have walked right past without recognizing it.

Somehow she spotted it in the dark.

"There it is!" Lea ran forward, stumbling as her toe hit a hunk of blackened rock and sent it flying.

"Ouch, ouch, ouch!" She hopped around holding her foot for a minute, swearing.

"Are you okay?" I asked, hurrying over.

"I'm fine. But that rock was hard.

"Isn't that usually the way with rocks?" Rustin teased.

My bestie glowered at the smart aleck shifter, her turquoise gaze glinting in the silvery light. "Alien rock is actually three parts metal and one part some other kind of ore. It's only called rock because that's what it was first mistaken for."

The "boulder" that was covered in the moss we'd been searching for was stained black like the night, the dense streaks and copious pockmarks likely the result of its volatile passage through the Earth's atmosphere.

Lea dropped to her knees beside the pile of regular rocks that had done a good job of nearly hiding it from view. Her hands hovered over the meteorite sticking up from the pile and she frowned, looking as if she were afraid to touch it.

"Is it volatile?" Grym asked, crouching down beside her and eyeing the black hunk of rock and metal.

"It's warmer than regular rock," Lea said. "This one is vibrating, can you hear it?"

We all fell quiet, hovering around the alien rock and listening.

"I hear a buzzing noise," Rustin said, frowning.

So did I. Lifting my gaze skyward, I spotted the Sprite buzzing past overhead. Sebille had changed into her fairy form earlier to scout the path ahead. When she saw us hunkered around the rock, she'd buzzed over to see what we were doing.

"It's just Sebille," I said, giving her a flat look.

"Oh," she said, her wings moving as fast as a hummingbird's. "Sorry." She transformed back into human form in a flash of pale green light.

We returned our attention back to the meteorite, and I finally heard a soft clanking sound as the alien rock vibrated against the ones surrounding it.

"Is that the moss?" I asked, eyeing the dull black coils covering the visible surface. As I stared at the stuff, I thought I saw it wriggle, like a bunch of earthworms in a jar.

"It is," Lea said, moving her hands closer. The moss began to glow orange, looking like banked coals in a grill.

Rustin, who'd been pressing his palms closer, suddenly jerked away with a hiss.

"What's wrong?" I asked.

"It burned my hands. Why is it heating up like that?" he asked Lea.

She shrugged. "No idea."

"We're going to have trouble getting it back to Croakies," he said.

"Can't you handle fire?" I teased. "You do breathe fire as your Chimera after all."

He didn't return my smile, frowning. "It's not like I have scales covering my entire body to protect me from fire."

"That's a big oversight on Maddie's part," Sebille groused.

"I'll let you tell her that," Rustin replied.

Leaves rustled nearby. I jerked my head up with alarm. It was hard not to think about all the nasties that liked to come out after dark in the mystical forest. When nothing jumped out at us, we returned to the problem of the moss.

"How are we going to harvest it if it's burning hot?" Sebille asked.

"And transport it," I added. "We should have brought Uncle Archie along with us. He could have made us a pocket void to carry it in."

They nodded their agreement.

I looked at Lea. "Can you make us a void?" She'd gotten pretty good at creating voids to stick naughty Baked Invaders and their friends into.

She shook her head. "I can make a void bubble with limited control over its movement, but I can't carry it long distances."

We fell into a thoughtful silence.

"It seems to be cooling down," Lea said a moment later. She risked touching it with a fingertip. "It's still pretty warm, but I think I can harvest the moss now. Pulling out the knife she'd brought for just that purpose, Lea gave the rock a tentative scrape beneath the coiled substance."

Flames shot up and flared wide, spewing a sulfuric stench in our direction.

We reared back with a variety of squeals and yelps, scattering.

"I don't think it liked your knife," Rustin said.

"You think?" Sebille asked, rolling her eyes.

A long, mournful howl stabbed the night around us. I swallowed hard, gooseflesh popping up along my arms. "Wolf."

"Werewolf," Grym and Rustin said at once.

Before I had a chance to wrap my mind around what that meant, the lone howler was joined by what sounded like a dozen others. "Not one werewolf," I breathed. "A whole pack of them."

"Great," Sebille muttered, popping back to fairy form. "That's just perfect." She buzzed off into the darkness, presumably to get more information about what we were about to face.

Either that...or she was hightailing it home and leaving us to deal with it ourselves. I didn't want to place bets on which of the two options it was.

Grym looked at Rustin. "I think this is a good time to shift."

Rustin nodded, looking unhappy about it. I didn't blame him. It seemed as if he was as much of a threat to his friends when he was the Chimera as he was to our enemies.

Lea motioned to the alien rock. "I'll work on getting us some of this moss."

I winced. "I'll...um...I'll just scream like a girl and run away."

Grym grinned, dropping a kiss to my forehead. "Good. We'll all be going with our strengths then."

I smacked his chest, which already felt like rock despite his still being in human form.

A familiar buzzing sound had me lifting my gaze skyward. Sebille did the equivalent of a skid on the air in front of us and flashed into full size. "At least a dozen of them. And they're wound up. This is going to be ugly."

"Awesome sauce," I murmured unhappily. "I don't suppose you know how to harvest some of this moss?" I asked my ever-helpful assistant.

Sebille blew a raspberry. "That's easy, give the knife to the gargoyle..."

A flash of nearby light informed of Grym's shift.

"...he's not flammable."

I wondered if that would still be true with the "more metal than rock" meteorite. "I'll guard Lea's back. You'll help the guys with the full moon set?"

She nodded. "I've already set a few traps for them."

Right on cue, a startled yelp filled the night. Followed by some angry snarling.

I held up a fist and the sprite bumped it with her own. Then she leaped into the air, turning bug-sized as she did, and flew back toward the cranky moon-bound puppies.

I perched on a large boulder near Lea, watching her weave a spell that she assured me should cause the moss to fall off the meteorite.

"Just fall off?" I asked skeptically.

"If it works right," she said, sounding only slightly confident.

"Maybe we can take the whole rock with us. The Meister should be able to harvest the moss. She's supposedly the queen of all things rock."

A low growl throbbed through the dark, the savage flavor of the sound making me shudder.

"I researched her and, despite her nasty personality, she does have a reputation for being good with rock," Lea said.

"That's good, because she's less fun to be around than that moss."

"Truth."

The distant snapping and snarling sounds were no longer all that distant. In fact, the battle had moved so near that I could hear bodies slamming into each other, and smell the musky scent of wolves.

I hadn't heard the oversized fracas I'd expected Rustin's Chimera to inspire, and realized he must be lying low. Picking off the low hanging fruit. I turned a worried gaze toward the sound of battle.

"They'll be okay," Lea assured me. Her long fingers danced on the air in front of her, the magic's soft green glow giving her a sickly hue. "Grym won't want to harm the wolves unnecessarily. They can be forgiven for a little moon madness right now. They did the right thing by coming into the Enchanted Forest, where they shouldn't have come up against humans or other benign creatures in the middle of the night."

I snorted out a laugh. "No smart ones, anyway. But that's actually what I'm worried about. Grym and Rustin are just trying to keep the wolves from hurting anybody. The wolves aren't going to be playing by the same rules. I'm betting that their whole plan for coming out on a full moon is to hurt and or eat something."

Lea's magic started to sizzle and swirl. She was too busy with the spell to respond.

Or to notice the long, lean shadow with the glowing gold eyes stepping slowly but confidently through the night.

By the time I saw him, the wolf was a mere ten feet away.

A distance a healthy male werewolf could cross in the blink of an eye.

Bees bosoms! I sent out a call to my favorite defensive artifact.

Moving slowly, I leaned forward and touched Lea on the shoulder. When she looked up with a question in her eyes, I spoke in a whisper. "Wolf, two o'clock."

The only warning I got was a hiss of displaced air, but my instincts had me lifting my hand just in time. The hilt of a sword hit my palm with a comforting smack, and the grip warmed and reshaped itself to fit neatly into my palm.

The spirit of a long-dead pirate fused with my own.

"Give way, ye scoundrel!" I yelled, the sword already tasting the air as I prepared to fight.

The werewolf leaped as I stepped between him and Lea. Oversized white fangs snapped as the beast sailed toward me, and I barely got the blade up in time to discourage him from striking. Landing a few feet away, the wolf snarled wetly, spittle spraying the area around his head and hitting the grass with a moist sizzle.

The wolf was a big one, probably weighing close to three hundred pounds, and if he managed to knock me to the ground, I wouldn't be getting up again. Not unless he wanted me to. And the slavering snarls that sent warm spittle over my face and arms told me the chances of that were slim.

The wolf's yellow gaze burned with feral power. An angry growl rumbled in the beast's chest as I swung Blackbeard's sword, smacking him hard in the face with the flat of the blade. The wolf dropped with a yelp but was up again with inhuman speed.

Behind me, Lea's magic thrummed and sparked, so close

to me that I felt the tiny scalds of it along my calves. "Lea, tell me you're almost done."

Barely managing to avoid the wolf's striking claws, I danced backward. I nearly fell as my heels came up against the pile of boulders.

"Five minutes," Lea said, her voice thrumming right along with her magic. "I'm working fast."

The wolf spun, his tail whipping as he loped away, and for a beat I thought he was leaving.

No such luck.

The creature disappeared into the shadows and I slid my gaze around the space, not knowing where he would come back out. A few frantic heartbeats later, the creature charged out of the woods from a different spot. He had circled around and I had to leap over Lea to get between them. I stumbled when I landed and was terrified he'd gain the advantage.

Jaw open as he snarled and snapped, the wolf leaped off the ground, sailing directly at me.

I didn't have time to react and had no choice but to duck, knowing it would probably be the end of me. If the beast managed to pin me to the ground when he hit, I wouldn't be able to gain my feet again before he savaged me. And even if I'd managed to strike, I'd probably injure Lea by mistake. She was just too close.

"Dastardly dog!" I yelled as I dropped, lifting Blackbeard's sword above my head and knowing I was going to have to hurt the werewolf more than I wanted in order to save Lea and myself.

"Bwawk!"

A bundle of ragged feathers rolled across the space between the wolf and me. The thing was a colorful tangle of beak, feathers, and talons and I barely kept the blade from giving the crazy parrot a feather trimming as he thrashed his way clumsily into the battle.

"Bleep ye scurvy bleeper and bleep yer mother too. When Blackbeard's sword ha' found ye, there's nothin' ye can do!"

"Be careful, SB," I yelled, drawing a few choice words from the foul-mouthed bird for my trouble. I winced as the wolf's jaws snapped within an inch of the big bird's moldy backside.

Somehow, SB—short for Sewer Beak for obvious reasons—managed to flounder and flap his way around the wolf, keeping between me and the befuddled creature through a combination of bluster, supernatural means, and sheer dumb luck.

"To the plank ye'll bleepin' go, and the bottom of the ocean ye'll see. 'Cause if Blackbeard's blade ha' ye in its sights, its edge will set ye free."

I let SB take most of the wolf's deadly attention and harried the beast when he was distracted. Don't judge! SB was already dead, and I hoped to survive the current battle in the opposite condition.

"Naida?" Lea called out, but the wolf chose that moment to attack with gusto. He leaped into the air and grabbed SB between his massive fangs. Lea gasped with horror, but a beat later, the wolf swung his head and sent the bird flying. He gagged and spit feathers from his mouth, looking as disgusted as I'd be if I'd chomped down on three pounds of moldy dead bird.

I used the distraction to move in and thrash the unfortunate creature with the flat of my blade, still hoping I could drive him away without really hurting him.

But alas, it was not to be. The werewolf swung his head and caught me unaware, sinking his teeth into my thigh.

I screamed and something ugly came over me. Pirate ugly. Blackbeard's ghost was displeased by the wolf's attack. The sword took over, controlling us both, and it became only a matter of time before the werewolf met the goddess face-to-muzzle.

I sprang into the deadly dance, some part of my mind aware that it wasn't what I wanted to do. But that part of me was no match for the spirit of a long-dead pirate and his favorite foul-mouthed bird.

SB flapped his way down to my shoulder and dug in his claws as I swayed and leaped, carving into the wolf with little restraint. "To bleep with ye blackguard!" SB squawked.

Not to be outdone, Blackbeard and I intoned, "Daft ye be, my barnacled foe. Dastardly and dense. Before ye taste this pirate's flesh, ye'll face dire recompense."

The wolf lunged, snarling.

"Ye and ye're bleepin' mother," SB added helpfully.

With a roar of deadly anticipation, I slashed at the wolf with the hungry blade, drawing blood.

The werewolf snapped his teeth, dangerously close to my throat.

SB laughed with glee. "Dance ye bleepin' barnacle bag. Dance with the devil's sword."

I feinted and the wolf fell into the trap, giving me a risky view of his tender throat.

"The scoundrel who waltzes the final waltz will pay the reaper's board."

I lunged, managing to keep the strike non-fatal, but just barely.

The wolf's answering yelp only drew the blade more eagerly into the dance, but I was fighting its influence with everything I had and my cuts were short, the stabs shallow. Still, the wolf was tiring. By the time he finally wearied of our battle and limped off into the woods, he was much worse off than he would have been if he hadn't taken first blood.

I sagged, feeling the poison of the artifact easing out of my system as I let the sword fall to the ground. I stumbled, hitting my knees and barely catching myself with a hand on the ground.

"Naida!" Lea was suddenly there, easing me into a seated position on the ground. She shook her head, her round face looking pale under the moonlight. "That was something else. I didn't know you could fight like that."

Panting with weariness, I shook my head. "That was all the sword." Swinging my hand vaguely in the direction of Croakies, I sent the blade away on a puff of air. I couldn't get far enough away from it, even though I'd likely need it again before we were safely back in the car.

SB took off after the sword, getting tangled in his own feathers as he went. His departure didn't do much for his hostile mood since he gave me one last verbal smack as he left. "Bleep yer mother's womb, ye bleepin' scoundrel!"

Beside me, Lea sighed. "Thank the goddess for that bleeping spell. I shudder to think what damage my tender psyche would take around that bird if it wasn't there."

"You and me both, girl."

11

NAKED YOGA ON THE NORTH POLE!

"What time is it?" I asked, wearily staring in the direction the others had gone. "Shouldn't they be back by now?"

Lea pulled out her phone and glanced at the face. "Two a.m." She frowned. "You're right, they should be here by now." She finished stuffing coils of severed moss into a toxic magic bag and slung it over her shoulder. "Should we go find them?"

I groaned as I shoved to my feet. Though Sebille had healed my wounds from the vulture attack, my whole body ached, and I couldn't stop a yelp of pain when I put weight on my injured leg.

Lea's eyes went wide. "Your leg! I'm so sorry, Naida. I forgot you were bitten. Let me heal it for you."

"It's okay. I think I can walk on it."

Lea gave me a flat look. "Don't be stupid," she scolded. "I know I don't heal as well as Sebille, but I can take the edge off the pain at least. She can finish healing it when we find her."

When we find her, I thought with a wince. What was

going on with Sebille and the two guys anyway? Where had they gone? Why hadn't they returned? "What could have happened to them?"

Lea motioned me to sit on a flat rock and shrugged. "Maybe they ran into more werewolves than expected."

Alarm stabbed through me. "They could be in a lot of danger," I said, trying to stand. "We need to find them."

She pushed me gently back down. "Not until I heal you."

I wanted to argue, but since I'd started moving around on my leg, the pain level had risen exponentially from what it had been when I was lying on my back on the cool ground.

Lea rustled in her bag and came up with a plastic baggie containing a damp rag. She pulled the rag out and draped it carefully over the bite mark, wrapping it tightly to keep it on the wound. "I won't ask you to drop your jeans out here." She gave me a wry grin. "So, this won't work as well as it normally would. Still, it should help some with the pain."

Unaccustomed anger tightened my chest and I took a long, quiet breath to alleviate it without Lea noticing. As I released it slowly, I forced a smile and thanked her. The leg started feeling better a few minutes later. "We should go now..." I started to say.

Lea held up a hand. "I want to do a spell for healing."

"Naked yoga on the North Pole!" I yelled in frustration.

Lea blinked in surprise, her mouth falling open. "Naida? What's wrong?"

I was breathing heavily, a cold sweat breaking out on my face as I battled the irrational emotion. "I just want to go check on the others. I'm worried about them. Aren't you worried?"

"Of course I'm worried. But I was trying to help you..."

"Okay, you helped. Now can we go? Please?"

Lea stared at me for a moment and then her expression tightened and she gave a curt nod. "Sorry for trying to help." She shoved to her feet and adjusted the bag containing the moss before taking off in the direction the others had gone, her long skirt flapping angrily around her boots.

I felt immediately sorry for my behavior. I didn't know what had come over me. I couldn't even remember why I'd gotten so mad.

Hurrying to catch up to Lea, I touched her arm. She yanked it away. I looked into her stormy turquoise gaze and winced. "You're right to be mad. I'm so sorry. I was awful."

"Yes. You were," she agreed in an irritated tone of voice.

"I'm really sorry."

"Whatever."

I winced again. It didn't seem like she was going to forgive me anytime soon. I realized I should just let her calm down and try to make it up to her later. With that decision made, I fell into step beside her, and we moved into the night under the weight of hurt feelings and anger.

We ended up walking nearly a mile before we found any sign of a battle.

A single white sneaker lay on its side in the path, the canvas upper dotted with blood.

I glanced around the small clearing where we stood. "Do you recognize that shoe? "I asked Lea. She was frowning, but I didn't think it was at me. "No. Do you think somebody else is in the forest tonight?"

"Either that or someone dropped their shoe out of a helicopter."

We shared a tentative grin.

"I'm not feeling very good about the blood," I told her.

"Maybe it's from a bloody nose."

"And somebody punched him right out of his shoe?"

She snorted. "It's possible."

I shone my flashlight toward the dirt around the shoe. There were signs of a scuffle, not too surprising, and...

"Those are paw prints." I told Lea. "Really big paw prints. You don't suppose...?"

"That the wolves carried somebody away?" The grim look she offered told me she did suppose that.

There were several other shoe prints and what looked like imprints from an animal that was larger than a wolf. "What do you suppose those are from?"

"Lion."

I blinked in surprise. "Like a mountain lion?"

"No. Like a rare, mythological creature that's part lion."

"Rustin's Chimera," I said, nodding. "They were here."

"It looks like it," Lea said. "Let's follow the trail and hopefully we'll find them."

Unfortunately, the trail led into the woods. It became much harder to follow the prints when the underbrush and root patterns obscured it. But Lea formed a tracking spell, based on the Chimera's very distinctive magic signature. She cast the spell, sending a small sphere blazing with yellow light bouncing along the ground ahead of us.

The thing moved quickly. Very quickly. I was out of breath after only a minute.

"Can you slow this thing down?" I asked, panting. My leg was throbbing but, after the way I'd behaved earlier, I really didn't want to tell Lea that.

She shook her head. "It paces itself according to how quickly the track was laid down. Apparently, Rustin was running."

Running. That sent my alarm bells ringing. What would a creature as terrifying as the Chimera be running from?

When I asked that question aloud, Lea said. "Maybe he was running after something."

Oh. Yeah. "You're good at this tracking stuff," I told my friend. Lea's manner hadn't warmed completely, but the chill she'd given off after I'd been a jerk had warmed a little. I was hoping a little flattery might make things toasty between us again.

Besides, it was the truth.

She shrugged, not looking at all like she felt flattered. "I've used my tracking skills to help find lost pets."

I nodded. I knew that. I'd forgotten. "Has someone ever lost a lion?" When she frowned a question at me, I grinned. "You knew right away that print was from the Chimera."

"Process of elimination. There aren't likely to be any other critters in this forest with that type of print and that size. Plus, I studied all kinds of animal prints when I started offering my tracking services."

Lea's little glowing orb bounced along at a wearying speed. My relief at being able to follow the path our friends had taken soon dulled as I fought roots and other stumble-causing vegetation while running through the dark.

Then we broke through to a clearing. A clearing I'd nearly missed because of the barrier formed by several broken trees littering the torn earth. The tree's shredded leaves and dented branches gave off a fresh green scent that told me they hadn't been on the ground for long.

That was my last thought before the little orb dove toward the ground and disappeared. Unfortunately, before I recognized what that meant, I had already stepped off the edge of the world, and plunged downward, into black, jagged nothingness.

My scream bounced against the jagged rock walls and came

back to me, sounding shrill. I tried to clamp my lips closed and stop screaming, but I couldn't seem to do it. The hole I'd fallen into went on and on, an endless terror that promised interminable agony when or if I found the bottom. That thought sharpened my screams and I gave up trying to stop. After all, it might be the last sound I'd ever be able to make.

12

INTERESTINGER AND
INTERESTINGER

I slammed down, the force of my landing yanking the air from my lungs and slicing off my hysterical screams. Before I had a chance to consider that I was still alive, hands grabbed my wrists and yanked me off the pile of relatively soft material I'd landed on.

Lea's screams ripped the air and cut off just as abruptly as mine as she hit the ground where I'd been.

Stress panting, I fought to calm down as Grym held me close, rubbing my back in comforting circles. He spoke softly into my ear, his voice taut with worry.

"I'm okay," I told him, pulling away.

"You're not okay," he said with a frown. Your leg is bleeding."

I tried to pull away. "Is Lea all right?"

"I'll live," my bestie said. But her voice sounded strained.

Rustin helped her sit up and glanced upward. "There's nobody with you?"

Lea shook her head. "We were following your trail."

"Yeah. We got worried when you didn't come back."

"We knew you'd follow us," Sebille said. "That's why we made that landing pad."

I glanced over to find a pile of jackets covering something green. "Is that...?"

"Moss," Sebille said, nodding. "It was the only thing we could find that's even marginally soft. Still, we weren't sure it would work. That's quite a fall."

Lea patted the moss bed. "This wasn't here when you guys fell?"

"No," Grym said, then smiled. "It's a good thing bumbles bounce."

Sebille snorted, the three of them sharing a secret.

"What does that mean?" I asked.

"He's talking about me," Rustin said. "I managed to shift and get my wings out just enough to slow my descent. They landed on me instead of the rocks."

I winced. "Ouch. You okay?"

"Nothing a stint with a psychiatrist won't fix."

Lea limped over. "Psychiatrist?"

"It appears the Chimera has a beast of burden complex. As in, he doesn't like people sitting on his back," Grym said with a grin.

"Not several hundred pounds of people, no." Rustin shifted his shoulders and grimaced. "You're no lightweight, derf."

"Do you need healing?" Lea asked, touching his arm.

"He's fine," Sebille said. "He's suffering phantom pain because he's a dink."

"I am not a dink. You try having a full-sized gargoyle land on your back. See how easily you walk it off."

I lifted my brows at Grym. "He's fat-shaming you."

"More like boulder shaming," the sprite said with glee.

Grym covered his heart with his hands. "I'm devastated."

A smile hovered on Rustin's lips and he shook his head.

"Can't you just shift a few times to heal?" Lea asked.

Lifting a dark brow, Rustin said, "Do you really want the Chimera going live in this small space?"

"Ah," she said. "Good point. I guess you're going to have to suck it up, buttercup."

"I get no respect," Rustin complained. "Besides, magic doesn't seem to work down here. Sebille can't go spritely and, once I reached the last ten feet or so of the plunge, my shifting magic gave out."

I thought about that for a beat, my panic taking flight again. If magic didn't work, we'd have to use mundane means to get ourselves back up to terrafirma. "So, what's the deal?" I asked. "What happened with the wolves?"

"They took off in this direction when they realized they were outclassed," Grym said with a frown. "The Chimera's prey drive kicked in and it went after them. We followed for fear that Rustin would eat a few of them if we didn't stop him."

Rustin frowned. "They jumped in front of me on the path. Do you know how dangerous that is?"

Sebille blew a raspberry. "You couldn't have caught me. I was in bug form."

"I was rock man," Grym said. "You'd have broken a few teeth on me."

Rustin shook his head. "We don't know if the wolves fell into this crevice or not. By the time we checked on them, they'd disappeared."

"And we ended up on the bottom of this stupid crevice," Grym finished.

"What about the owner of the lost sneaker?"

The three of them looked at Lea, their faces blank.

"Huh?" Sebille said.

I frowned. "You didn't see the shoe?"

They shook their heads. I looked at Lea. From her expression, I deduced she was thinking what I was thinking. "Somebody else is in these woods."

"Or *was*, at least," Lea said. "There was blood on that sneaker."

"Is it my imagination," I asked hours later, "or is this crevice getting deeper?"

Lea swiped her forearm over her sweaty brow. "I'm pretty sure we're going to step into a puddle of the earth's molten core any minute."

"Are we sure we're going the right way?" Rustin asked.

"I'm sure," Grym said, his expression mulish. "You've asked me that a million times."

"It's just that..." He threw me a look as if asking for help. I pretended I didn't see it. "We've been walking for a long time. Maybe we should have gone the other way."

"I've lived my entire life in Enchanted," Grym said. "I used to play in this forest when I was a kid."

I blinked in surprise but Sebille beat me to the punchline. "Your parents didn't like you much, huh?"

Grym sighed. "Not too much can hurt a gargoyle."

Maybe not, I thought. But lots of things in the Enchanted Forest had tried.

"The sky's getting lighter," Lea said, her voice sounding hopeful. I didn't know why she'd be hopeful since all the light in the world wouldn't get us closer to the surface.

I pulled my cell phone out of the back pocket of my jeans. One glance told me we were still out of luck.

"Do you have a cell?" Rustin asked hopefully. There

seemed to be a lot of that going around. I only wished I had some hopefulness myself.

"Nothing. I guess the earth's core doesn't support 5G."

Sebille snorted.

"I guess the wolves didn't fall into the crevice."

We all turned to Lea. She sounded tired and her hopefulness seemed to have disappeared. When she saw us looking, she explained. "There's no place they could hide in this crack."

"Maybe they went the other way," Rustin said, throwing Grym a narrow-eyed gaze.

"*Holy flippin' frog flatulence!*" Grym exclaimed, throwing up his arms. "Do you want to turn around and go the other way?"

"It's a little late for that now, isn't it?" Rustin replied.

"You could have said something when we were making the decision. But no. You went all passive aggressive and waited until we'd committed before you started whining."

Rustin growled, his aura spitting silver sparks that were the precursor to his change.

"Rustin," I said, stepping backward and pulling Lea with me. I jerked my head for Sebille to move away from Rustin just in case.

Grym clenched his fists and started to swell. The distinctive sound of ripping fabric came from his strained clothing as he swelled into his gargoyle.

"Stop it, you two!" I yelled. They ignored me and I was horrified to see Rustin's aura taking the shape of the Chimera. He was seconds from shifting.

"I mean it, you two. Stop it right now!"

Grym's skin took on a grayish quality, fine veining running through the rocky form of his gargoyle.

Sebille made a sound like a sob. My head whipped

around and my mouth fell open when I saw that she was crying. Crying! Sebille! "What's wrong with you?" I asked, on the verge of losing my stuffing too.

"Grym's frog swear reminded me of Slimy. What if the little guy's really sick? We're not there to help him."

Lea wailed in my ear and I jumped, smacking my head on the rocky wall. "Now what?"

"I was supposed to give him his second dose of medicine hoooouuuurrrrs ago," she wailed pathetically.

Grym's shift stopped as he stared at the two women.

I smacked him on the arm and then yelped as my fingers nearly broke.

"What was that for?" he asked in his growly gargoyle voice.

"You said frog and set them off." It was getting harder to ignore that the cracking artifact appeared to be affecting more than just Croakies' floor and walls.

A puff of smoke tickled my nostrils and my head snapped around to find the Chimera standing there, smoke wafting from its lion nostrils.

"Jeezopete," I murmured. "Don't anybody move."

Lea stopped mid-wail and Sebille made a disturbing honking sound.

The Chimera's tooth-filled maw opened and it roared.

I glared at Sebille, who'd just noisily blown her nose after I'd told her to be still.

She frowned at me. "You didn't say to be quiet. Just to be still."

"Goddess help me." I tried to smile at Rustin. Even I could tell the taut curve of lips was probably more scary than soothing. "Hey buddy. You want to pack that away and come back to us now? Pretty please?"

A growl rumbled through the creature's massive body.

I didn't turn my head to look at Grym as I spoke. "You got any ideas?"

"Um...here kitty, kitty?"

Sebille snorted.

Lea sniffled.

I sighed. "If we don't move or *make noise*," I said softly. "Maybe he'll revert back to human from sheer boredom."

"That works for me," Grym said, not sounding too concerned. He'd finished his change into the gargoyle and was impervious to almost everything.

I growled a little in my throat. "You're lucky I can't move right now or I'd be all up in your grill."

"That sounds interesting," he purred.

"It won't be. Unless you're into pain."

"Interestinger and interestinger."

Ugh.

"Woof!"

At first I thought I'd imagined it, but then the Chimera turned its head in the direction of the sound. The creature roared, fire flaring from its maw along with the bellow. Grym jumped away from the fire before realizing he was currently made of rock.

"Was that..." I started to ask.

Rustin spun on his paws and took off running down the crevice.

I took off after him, having no idea what I'd do if I caught up to him. The three stooges thundered after me, likely with even less of an idea for what to do than I had.

"Woof!"

"It couldn't be," Grym said, catching up to me. "We left her at Croakies."

I didn't respond since, unlike the gargoyle, I wasn't in tip top shape and would likely fall over and die with my legs and arms in the air like a cockroach if I expended the air to talk. But I thought a response. *Just because we left the demon dog at home, doesn't mean she'll stay there.*

Not surprisingly, Grym didn't respond, since he couldn't read my mind.

13

A WEREWOLF IN LONDON

"Woof!" The sound of an approaching dog was getting closer. I wouldn't have expected that a barking dog would affect our problem one way or the other, except that, if it truly *was* Vel, my little green demon dog, she could endanger us with her magically enhanced barking.

"Is that her?" Sebille asked. "It sounds like her."

Another heartfelt "Woof!" made the ground around us tremble, and rocks came loose on the crevice's walls. I covered my head as they tumbled down around us, escaping a concussion when Grym shielded me with his big body. He urged Lea and Sebille to join the huddle, and did what he could to protect us from sharp, flying rocks.

Rustin stopped running and let out a roar as rocks tumbled down around him.

"I think it's her," I said with mixed emotions. On the one hand, I'd be glad to see the little dog and maybe she could help. On the other hand, she was just one little dog inside the Universe's most deadly magical forest.

But our problems were about to get worse.

"Hopefully she won't run into the wolves," Lea said, "Meow!"

Lea and I shared a horrified glance.

I looked up, up, and up to the top of the fissure high above. A small gray face appeared, and Wicked pawed the edge, looking as if he was going to jump.

"No, Wicked!" I screamed.

Lea made a choked sound.

"Aawooooooooooo."

"There are the wolves! Grym!"

He swore softly. "Let me try something." Without warning, he backed up to the opposite wall of the crevice, dug in his toes, and took off at a sprint. He leaped as he reached the wall, his fingers finding the jagged rock and digging in. Dust and small rocks tumbled down the wall as Grym made his own finger and toe holds in the stone.

Watching him climb, I forgot to breathe. But it wasn't until a small green head appeared at the top of the crevice, joining the even smaller gray one, that I truly lost my cool. "Hurry, Grym," I said.

"Aawooooooooooo."

"The wolves sound a lot closer."

To his credit, he didn't yell back at me, though he'd have been justified. He was climbing steadily, but not very quickly. He'd reached an area where the ground jutted and he was having trouble getting a handhold since the dirt-to-rock ratio was weighted more heavily toward dirt.

And dirt crumbles. Especially with three hundred pounds of rock man hanging from it.

Vel whined pitifully. I looked up at the little dog. "I know, girl. It's okay. We're going to get out of here. Just sit tight."

"Aawooooooooooo."

Chills ran up my spine at the feral sound of the

approaching wolves. I bit my lip and paced, knowing Wicked and Vel were in real danger.

"That sounded really close," Lea said.

"Close, yeah," Sebille frowned. "I think we have a problem, ladies."

I didn't even look at her. My gaze was locked on Grym and the fur babies.

But Lea swallowed audibly and she reached out to clutch my arm. "Naida, I think you need to see this."

I fought the urge to shake her off. "Just a minute."

"No," she said, her voice tight. "Now."

I expelled a frustrated breath and spun on her. "What? I can only handle one crisis at a time."

But she didn't respond. She was gazing with wide eyes at the space behind us. For a beat, I didn't comprehend what I was looking at. It was just too weird. And horrifying.

Then it clicked, and I grabbed Lea's wrist, dragging her backward as all three of us continued to gawk.

"What is it?" Grym asked. I knew I couldn't tell him, because he needed to stay focused on what he was doing. But, galloping gargoyles! I really wanted to. "Just a small problem. Keep doing what you're doing. We'll handle it."

"Are you sure? I can..." The sound of dirt and rock tumbling down the wall made me throw up a hand. "I'm sure. Concentrate on what you're doing."

"Aawoooooooooo."

The force of the howl just about blew the hair back from my face. We stepped backward and put up our hands in a defensive move. Not that our hands would do anything against...

"What is it?" Lea asked.

"Unnatural and unacceptable," Sebille said. She screwed up her face, looking like she had gas.

"What are you doing?" I asked, kicking myself for getting distracted by her antics.

"Trying to go buggy. Why could Grym and Rustin shift down here, but I can't."

"Your other form is just you, only smaller. They actually changed. Maybe that's why?" Lea suggested.

"That doesn't make any sense," Sebille crabbed.

"I'm open to hearing a better suggestion," Lea crabbed right back.

"Okay, you two. Zip it. We have a situation here."

"Ya think?" Sebille snarked.

"Anybody got any weapons?" I asked quietly, as if the thing standing further up the crevice from us could hear and understand me. Maybe it could. Who the heck knew? The entire world appeared to be irredeemably cracked.

"Rocks," Sebille offered dryly. "We have lots of those."

"Oh, I see a stick," Lea said. Forgetting herself, she lunged for a branch on the ground, moving too quickly.

The thing growled, the sound so deep it vibrated against my skin.

Lea ground to a halt.

"White whiskered weasels," Grym ground out. "What on the goddess's green earth is that?" He was at the top of the crevice...thank the goddess...and he looked ready to jump back down.

The creature we were all gaping at stood well over six feet tall, with bloodshot red eyes and fangs the length of my pinkie fingers. Its features were mostly human, but its nose had darkened to a purple black and looked moist, like a dog's.

Golden fur covered its visible flesh, longer and thicker at the top and swept back with a noticeable widow's peak between bushy brown brows.

Its tongue was black and hung out one side, like a goofy dog and just as drooly.

"It's wearing Sebille clothes," Lea muttered beside me.

She wasn't wrong. The creature had on bell-bottomed pants that sported wide navy stripes, and a Hawaiian shirt that was a riot of flowers and palm leaves. The combination was seizure inducing.

It...he...wore one white sneaker, his unshod foot covered in fur with inch-long black claws that curved into the ground where it stood.

The entire time we stood there looking at him, a low growl vibrated in his throat.

"What's the plan?" Grym asked, sounding as if he was going to come up with one of his own if somebody didn't beat him to it.

I risked a glance up. "We're open to suggestions," I said, trying to sound calm.

"Is that what was howling before?" he asked.

"It seems the great protector has more questions for us than answers," Sebille snarked.

"Give me a minute. I'm trying to get up to speed here."

"Suggestions?" I repeated.

"Um. Okay. Move very slowly. In fact, don't move at all, unless it moves. Then run like you have a racecar engine in your drawers."

Sebille snorted. "Helpful."

"I'm coming back down," Grym said.

"No! Our only hope of getting out of here is you. Go find a vine we can use as a rope and leave this to us."

"Not a chance, Naida. That thing is nasty. It could kill you with one bite."

Sebille screwed up her face. "Are you sure? If you narrow your eyes to slits, he looks kind of cute."

We all turned slow glances her way.

When she saw us all staring she said, "What?"

"You need to date more," Grym said.

Sebille sniffed. "Whatever."

"Woof!"

"No, Vel. You stay up there. You're going to get..." The little dog jumped off the ground, her mouth opening.

Wooooooooofffffff...

Grym leaped in Vel's direction, hands outstretched to grab the little green pup. I called out to stop them, but the words got lost in the force of Vel's magic and were unraveled, drifting like cloudy swirls through the thickened air.

The world twisted and bent. The walls around me rolled like an amusement park ride and rocks flew away from them, flying straight up rather than down as gravity should have determined. A weird screeching sound drew me from a surprised haze and I looked around, fearing the whole crevice was going to land on top of us.

That was when I realized the screeching came from the odd, wolfy creature. It had fallen to its knees and was tugging on its perfect hair, bloodshot eyes filled with pain.

I took a step in its direction, but the ground beneath my feet rumbled and split, the surface dropping out from under me. I plunged downward, screams and the sound of breaking rock lighting up the early morning quiet.

I clawed at the wall, trying to stop the fall by grabbing onto anything I could reach. But my fingernails broke and tore and handholds disintegrated under my desperate grasp.

The split kept deepening, and I fell, and fell, and fell, and...finally stopped falling. I didn't hit bottom, but I was suddenly standing on the air, and the sound of the earth splitting had stopped. Dizziness swamped me, my head giving a couple of really painful throbs, and I supported myself against the wall for a minute, breathing deeply until a wave of nausea broke.

"Um...Can anybody hear me?" I called after a minute. Even to me, my voice sounded broken.

"Naida? Thank the goddess! You're okay?" Grym's voice sounded far, far away.

"Bad girl," Sebille scolded.

I thought about defending myself. "I'm not a bad girl," I muttered unhappily.

"Very bad," Sebille said.

Vel whimpered.

"Don't scold her Sebille. I'm not sure what her whining might do. Magically speaking."

"Naida," Grym called out. "Don't worry, we're going to get you out of there."

There, being a deeper crevice inside a deep crevice. Peachy. Nobody could ever say my life was boring. "Is everybody else okay?" I yelled.

There was only a slight hesitation before Grym said, "Yeah. Mostly."

"That didn't sound very convincing," I said. "Who's hurt?" I tested the surface I stood on, wondering if it would move up with me if I tried to climb. It didn't budge.

"Well, the werewolf guy bent a finger."

I stopped trying to climb. "He...um...spoke to you?"

"Yeah. He's a nice guy. I think," Grym said.

"I'm London," an unfamiliar voice with a British accent said. "Nice to meet you."

I considered and rejected several snarky comebacks before saying. "Go ahead, Sebille."

"The werewolf was *in* London," the sprite said with obvious delight.

A series of snorts followed.

"There, do you feel better now that you've gotten that out?" I asked the sprite, fighting a grin myself.

"I do. Thanks."

"Wanker," London groused.

"I won't ask you how the werewolf got in you...London," I said, choking back a laugh.

Snorts transformed to snickers and guffaws above me.

"Not until we're all out of here and safe."

"Much appreciated."

I tried digging my fingertips into the wall again but pain slashed through them from the torn nails so I stopped. "What's the plan for getting me out of here?"

"You won't like it," Lea said.

"I wouldn't be so sure. I'd probably do just about anything right now. Talk to me."

"Well, we have good news and bad news."

I cringed. "Okay."

"The good news is that Vel's bark magic filled the crack in at one spot so everybody could climb out."

"That *is* good news."

Silence.

More silence.

"And what's the bad news?"

"Ah. Well," Grym cleared his throat and gave an uncomfortable laugh. "Don't freak out. I mean...it's probably nothing serious..."

"Oh for sinners' sake," Sebille said, "Your cat is glowing and floating six inches above the ground."

Son of a donkey.

14

GUYS, I THINK THIS CRACK IS IMPLODING

"Ah!"

Lea's scream jolted me out of my frantic thoughts and concerns about Wicked. "What? What's happened? Is Wicked okay?"

"He's fine, Naida," Sebille said in her, "You've just stepped on my last nerve" voice. "A bunch of naked men just walked up on us."

I blinked, my mind swirling and spinning. "Naked men? I...um...assume it's the missing werewolves?"

Rustin's face appeared at the top of the crevice. It surprised me because I hadn't realized the top was visible until that moment. Well, sort of visible. Rustin looked really small and far away.

"Hey! Are you naked?" I asked him.

He shoved his glasses up his nose. "What a strange question."

"Sebille said a bunch of naked men just showed up." Shrugging and pink of cheeks, I slammed my lips together as embarrassment swamped me.

"I am not. As it happens, I shift back fully clothed."

"And thank the goddess for that," Grym rumbled.

"But these other guys..." Sebille said, a grin in her voice. "Boys, say hi to Naida."

There was some flesh-colored shuffling around the top of the hole and I yelped, closing my eyes and using my hands as barriers just in case. "Nope. That's okay. I don't need to say hello to anybody who isn't wearing clothes."

Sebille snorted. "prude".

"I am not a prude. Tell her, Lea."

Silence.

"Lea?"

Indistinct burbling sounds followed. I assumed they represented Lea's brain melting down.

A strange face appeared over the edge. "Hi, Naida. It's London, the werewolf."

"Hi werewolf in London," I said, stifling a laugh. "Did you know they named a cult classic after you?"

Titters followed that observation.

"I am aware." He frowned, but went on to explain. "We found a vine. We're going to lower it down to you in just a few minutes. Grym's tying two vines together so they'll be long enough to reach you."

Rocks sifted down the sides of the crevice. A mid-sized one landed on my toes and I bit back a yelp, not wanting to alarm anybody. But the slight feeling of claustrophobia I'd had since falling into the hole worsened. Stars burst before my eyes and a cold sweat broke out on my forehead. "Can somebody please keep talking to me?"

I would have given anything in that moment to be able to pace. But I was afraid to move for fear the whole thing would come down on my head.

"Woof!" Vel's cute green head appeared at the edge and

her body shook from side to side, like it did when she was wagging her tail especially hard.

"Not you, little girl," I said. "You've done enough damage today."

"Woof!" she replied happily,

"Hey, guys," Lea said, her voice semi-calm. "What's Wicked doing?"

"He's just trying to get away from the naked were-wolves," Sebille responded.

"Here kitty, kitty," an unfamiliar, deep voice said.

"My, my, gramma. What big teeth you have," Another unfamiliar voice joked.

"Is he still glowing and floating?" I asked, afraid to hear the answer.

"Um…"

I dropped my face into my hands and swore silently.

"Wait! No!"

There was a soft thud, like something big hitting the ground above my head, and more rocks filtered down onto me. I cried out at the pain. A beat later, I looked down to find my feet buried in dirt and rocks. Not good.

"Guys, I think this crack is imploding." A shadow fell over the hole.

"Meow."

My gaze jerked upward and I gasped as I spotted what had to be the strangest sight so far in a totally cracked day.

Wicked was floating calmly down to me, an eerie yellow glow surrounding him. "Buddy? What are you doing?"

"Meow!" he repeated, his tail snapping the air.

I held out my arms and he settled into them, his soft warmth going a long way toward calming my jangled nerves. Burying my face in his fur, I took two deep breaths and slowly released them.

I felt immediately calmer. Until I remembered I was no closer to being released from the deep fissure. And Wicked was in danger too.

I opened my mouth to ask how long it would be before the vine was ready. But the words never emerged.

"Woof!" My small green dog leaped into the hole and plummeted toward Wicked and me. "Vel!" I managed before she slammed into us...and the surface beneath my feet gave way.

We plunged fast enough to yank the breath from my lungs, and my brain locked up under a wave of pure terror. As we passed through layer upon layer of rock and dirt and stuff that sparkled and shone with an odd light, I was vaguely aware of Wicked still purring and Vel licking my cheeks.

It was surreal.

I had well and truly fallen down the rabbit hole and was heading for Wonderland.

Blithering bat boogers!

THE SULFUROUS STENCH was the first thing that hit me.

The ground was the second thing.

I slammed into the hard, uncomfortably hot floor with the force of a cannon-ball slamming into a mountainside. Agony speared up my back from the impact and my bones felt as if they were grinding together.

I expected to be three inches shorter when I stood up. *If* I stood up. The way my body was creaking and groaning, I wasn't sure being ambulatory was in my future.

Mr. Wicked jumped off my lap, plopped himself on the

heated rock floor, and proceeded to bathe his plus-sized belly with a contented and unrelenting purr.

Vel scampered away, tail happily wagging and tongue dangling wetly from the side of her mouth.

I rubbed my sacroiliac and wished for a tall iced tea with lemon. "It was thoughtful of you both to let my poor boohind take the brunt of our landing."

Mr. Wicked made a whirring sound and gave me soft eyes. Vel's tail whipped harder.

Rolling to my knees, I groaned to a halt. Before standing, I needed to wait for my freshly compacted spine to cease and desist its temper tantrum.

"Woof!"

I straightened in a panic, regretting it immediately. "Vel, no barking!"

The pup glanced back at me, still grinning. Her full-body wriggle told me she was not cowed by my tone. "Please don't bark. Okay, sweetie?"

She bounced joyfully and dropped into play position.

"Sorry, girl. We'll have to play later. Right now I have two problems. First, I'm currently crippled. Second..." I looked around with despair. "I need to figure out how to get out of here, wherever *here* is, and get us home."

I was unprepared for the whir of movement slashing in our direction, and barely had time to fling up my hands before it slammed into me.

"Miss!" the source of the whir screamed into my face. "Please help me. Baca's in danger!"

"Hobs? What...? Where...?"

The hobgoblin grabbed my hand. "Please, miss. You have to save her."

I opened my mouth to ask questions, but his spidery

fingers tightened on mine and he shot away, pulling me helplessly along with him. We stopped so suddenly that I kept flying for a beat, nearly slamming into something solid and smooth before Hobs stopped me with a yank on my arm.

"Ugh!" I said as pain ricocheted up my arm and stabbed my twisted shoulder. My poor, battered backside slammed down last. I groaned in pain. "Hobs, don't just yank me around like that. I'm not as resilient as you."

"Sorry, Miss. But Baca really needs your help."

I was flattered by his confidence in me. But I doubted there was anything I could do to help the little brownie in the...earth's core? I glanced around, my eyes slowly adjusting to what looked like a cave, the walls striped with ore and sparkling with something that looked like diamonds. Several yards away, a bubbling pool of something spit and splashed against the rocky formations sticking up from the cave's floor and hanging down from its ceiling.

In some places the hot liquid had melted holes in the stalagmites, leaving sulfurous steam behind to fill the space.

Was that the lacy rock we needed to harvest?

"Where is she, Hobs?" I asked, my gaze sliding toward the boiling pool as dread twisted my stomach.

"Right there, Miss."

I dragged my gaze in the direction he was pointing.

The wall I'd nearly hit when I'd landed was a golden color, smooth with internal pocks. It appeared to be partially transparent, and something moved behind the golden surface. I twitched in surprise as I realized that it was a face. "Baca?"

"Yes, Miss," Hobs said. The little brownie probably couldn't hear me from behind that rock. "She fell in there somehow. I don't know how. I've looked all over this cave and there's nothing. No opening at all."

Tears slipped down his cheeks. His entire body trembled and his liquid blue gaze was locked on the face behind what looked like yellow glass. *Thick*, yellow glass.

I splayed my hand on the surface of the stuff, noting that it was warm but not hot. I pounded it with my fist and there was no sound. It also didn't seem in any danger of breaking. "What is this stuff?" I mumbled.

"Amber, Miss."

I turned to him with a frown. "Amber? At the earth's core?"

"We're not quite at the core, Miss," Hobs said. "The Meister sent us here."

"And where is *here*, exactly?" I asked, glancing around for clues.

"Beneath the Enchanted Forest. Way beneath it," he said. "But not as deep as the inner or outer core. She said the rock we're searching for is too fragile to survive the pressures of the inner core. Since the outer core is liquid, the rock would turn to magma there."

"Okay, so how did Amber get this deep under the surface?"

"I don't know, Miss. I'm guessing the crack allowed it to sink."

"That's plausible, I guess." I pressed my face to the amber wall to see if I could make out the stone surrounding Baca's unfortunate prison. With all the air bubbles and debris caught in the amber, it was hard to see much, but the color of the back wall seemed to imply that it might be limestone.

The little brownie placed her hand against the wall where mine was and my heart broke a little. She was likely terrified. I pressed closer to the wall and yelled so she could hear me. "We're going to get you out, Baca," I said, trying to sound confident. She hesitated a beat as if trying to decide if she believed me, and then gave her head a quick nod.

"She's really scared, Miss," Hobs said, his voice thick with unshed tears.

"I know. We're going to get her out."

"Woof!"

I whipped around, finding Vel standing a few feet away, her eyes bright with intent. I had no idea how she could have found us, but I'd learned to expect the impossible with the little magical dog. Tapping my lips with a finger, I said, "Shh. No barking, Vel. Remember?"

She wagged her tail harder.

"What are we going to do?" Hobs asked, wringing his long, skinny fingers.

Shaking my head, I said, "I don't know. Give me a minute to think." I tried to remember my science classes on melting points. Maybe we could use the bubbling liquid in the pool to melt the wall of amber. Or at least soften it so we could bust Baca out.

I walked closer to the bubbling liquid, wondering what it was. It looked like water but it had a sulfuric stench. "I'll bet this is a hot spring." With that realization, I suddenly knew where we were. Or, more specifically. What we were under. There was a hot springs park on the furthest Western boundary of the Enchanted Forest. The area wasn't a popular tourist spot, and tended to be forgotten because the springs were far too hot for anyone to use. In fact, there was generally at least one death reported at the springs every year.

I hadn't known there was a cave system beneath the springs, and the thought didn't make me feel very safe. One touch of that water would create a serious burn. Falling into it was certain death. Assuming I could use the heat to melt the amber wall, how would I transfer it there without being burned to the bone?

"Woof!"

"No, Vel! Bad girl."

I jumped as a loud cracking sound filled the cavern where we stood. My eyes quickly found the spot and I grimaced as I realized the wall above Baca's prison was cracking. I glared at Vel. "Did you do that?"

She gave me her best innocent look.

"Miss! That's good. If the wall breaks Baca can get out."

I shook my head. I didn't want to scare him any more than he already was, but that breaking rock was more likely to land on top of Baca than set her free. Another loud crack had me backing up, pulling Hobs with me and calling Vel to us. "I'm afraid the chances of her escaping before that wall lands on her aren't good."

And if the large chunks of rock landed in the spring, we were in danger of being scalded by the splashes.

As if conjured by my thoughts, a large chunk of the wall behind Baca broke off and rolled into one of the rocky protrusions on the cavern floor, sending it into the hot spring in a geyser of sizzling liquid.

I sucked in a pained gasp as tiny splashes sizzled against my exposed flesh. Hobs cried out too, and we moved as far from the water as we could.

The cavern fell still for a beat, but our reprieve didn't last long. The whisper of thousands of tiny feet made my stomach twist with fear. As thousands of thumbnail-sized spiders boiled out of the hole made by the broken wall, and headed right for us.

15

CRAAAAACCCCCKKKKK

A shrill scream ripped my horrified gaze to Baca. Through the cloudy amber separating us, I could see the little brownie leaping around, slapping at something all over her clothes.

"The spiders got to Baca!" Hobs screamed. He took off toward his friend before I could stop him.

I reached for him but missed him by inches. "Hobs, wait. There could be more rocks collapsing."

He leaped onto a pile of fallen rock, setting another small avalanche into motion. The scalding liquid in the pool spit scorching globules into the air that sizzled against his clothing.

He didn't seem to notice.

"Baca!" he screamed, frantic to get to her.

Something tickled my legs and arms. I looked down to find dozens of furry black bodies marching over my shoes and climbing up my jeans. A slithery feeling beneath my clothes told me they'd gotten under the fabric too.

I freaked out, leaping and flailing around, trying to rid myself of the nasty critters any way I could. Pain slashed my calves and gnawed my belly. The nasty creatures were biting me.

"Ah!" I screamed, nearly tempted to leap into the steaming water just to get rid of them.

"Wooooooffffffff!"

Vel's bark swept power through the room, abrading the air like sandpaper and creating a floating sensation that made me imagine, for just a moment, that I was light enough to fly.

I turned to my dog just as Vel left the ground. Like Wicked had done back at the collapsed crevice, the little dog levitated into the air, her bright black eyes round with intrigue. She seemed to be grinning, and she was making happy little woo-woo sounds.

"What's happening?" I asked my sidekick, then yelped as my feet left the ground too. "Vel!" panic started my legs and arms flailing, and sent me into a spin that threatened to run me into the walls or ceiling of the cavern. Fighting the loss of control, I made it worse and the spinning sped up.

Hobs, literally, flew past me and crashed into Vel. I reached for them, spinning past, out of control.

With a shout of horror, I found myself dangling above the bubbling spring. Though I fought to move away from it, I somehow only managed to move closer.

I spun faster. And faster. Until the walls of the cavern were a blur.

Hobs spun past. At least, I thought it was Hobs since he was spinning too fast to identify.

Then, to my horror, I realized the water in the pool was rising, forming a funnel and lifting into the air.

The wall behind Baca's prison groaned mightily, and more huge chunks bounced off the rocky ceiling of her prison, slamming down to the cavern floor. The fall spewed dust and tiny projectiles of rock around the space.

The projectiles got caught in the spinning water and shot from the funnel like bullets.

Pain slashed my cheek, then my throat, and another projectile sliced into my forearm. They were relentless.

"Vel!" I screamed. "Stop!"

But the chaos didn't stop. I realized a moment later that the water spout was heading toward Baca's amber prison.

Was that what the little demon dog was trying to do? Was she trying to melt the amber? And, more importantly, had she read that idea in my mind?

Ugh!

"Vel!!!" I screamed again as a thunderous roar filled the cavern. Chunks were coming off the walls and ceiling faster and faster. Some of the bigger chunks were getting caught in the whirlwind and shooting across the room like deadly projectiles.

I folded myself into a ball like a fuzzy caterpillar and tried to protect my important parts as I was pelted from all directions. A heavy splash had me unrolling slightly, to see what was going on.

The pool water had hit the amber wall, but rather than melting the amber, it had set it on fire!

"Blithering baboon buttocks! Vel!"

She whined.

Just like *that*, the rocks in the air stopped spinning and hit the ground.

The water fell back into the pool.

The walls of the cavern ceased disintegrating.

And I had a cartoon-like moment where I hung in the air with a horrified expression on my face for a second before plunging like lead in maximum gravity and smashing against the debris-strewn ground.

A second thud sounded as Hobs hit the ground with me. Baca's tiny form barely made a noise as she landed inside her fiery prison.

As we lay there groaning in pain and dizziness, a final long "craaaaaccccckkkkk" sliced the air and the cavern went quiet.

Baca stepped through the new breach in her prison and looked around, absently scratching spider bites on one skinny arm.

Vel floated gently down to earth, looking smug as only a dog can. "Woof!" she said happily.

"I got your woof right here, little miss," I grumbled.

She woo-wooed again, black eyes sparkling.

Hobs jumped up and ran over to a small niche at the bottom of a wall that was far away from the pool. Pulling a large canvas bag out of it, he unzipped the top and showed it to me. Filigreed rock half-filled the bag.

"Good," I said. "Nice work. How'd you cut all that?"

"Baca has a special blade," he said with a smile toward his friend.

The brownie's cheeks pinkened with pleasure.

Nodding, I forced myself to look around. I needed to figure out how to get us out of there.

"Naida?" Grym's voice was filled with astonishment. "What's going on down there?"

My eyes popped open and I found myself looking up, up, up through a sunken hole inside another massive crevice. "The whole world is cracked," I said, except that the word had taken on a whole new meaning. I shoved gingerly to my feet and looked around.

There was a fresh new crack severing the little cavern with the superheated pool.

Baca's prison had been eviscerated, the amber still smoking and a new breach slicing through the very center. Spider bodies littered the ground.

I tugged the collar of my shirt out and looked down at myself, suddenly feeling as if tiny feet were traipsing all over me. But they were all dead. Shuddering and quaking, I tried to shake the nasty corpses loose.

"Um, Naida?" Grym said, lifting a dark eyebrow at my inappropriate behavior.

"Sorry. There were spiders," I said.

"Lots and lots of spiders," Hobs agreed.

"Soooooo many spiders," Baca concurred.

"Can you maybe get us out of here?" I asked him, my voice breaking on the last word.

His expression softened. "Sure. We called the fire department. There are ladders coming. They should be here in five minutes."

I took a deep breath and let it go. "Good. That's good."

"Meow!"

Soft, warm fur slipped over my ankles and an immediate sense of calm sifted through me. I reached down and scooped up my cat, burying my face in his fur. "Hey, buddy. Thanks for coming to make me feel better."

"Meow," he rubbed his face over mine, purring loudly.

"How'd you guys get under the springs?" Rustin asked.

I looked up to find that the others had joined the circle of faces high above. I waved at everyone, trying on a weary grin. "It's a long story, which I won't have the energy to tell until I've had half a dozen egg rolls and some ice cream."

They chuckled as I'd known they would. "The bigger question is how you found us again."

Lea pointed toward Wicked. "Your magical kitty told us where you'd be."

"Told you?" I asked, frowning. Had I missed my cat's first words? A wave of sadness swept me. Ever since Mr. Slimy had started talking into my mind, I'd clung to the hope that Wicked would do the same thing someday. It would be terrible if I missed it when he did.

"Well, actually, he just took off running and we ran after him. I knew you'd be beside yourself when you got out of that hole if he was lost." My bestie shook her head. "I have to admit, I didn't expect to find you at the bottom of another crevice."

"It seems that's all there is anymore. Cracks upon cracks upon cracks." As I had that thought, I realized I was afraid to go back to Croakies. We'd been gone for hours. How bad would the crack there be? And Mr. Slimy... Panic swelled. "Has anybody checked on Slimy?"

"Sebille went home about an hour ago. She was going to give Slimy his meds and see how the Rock Meister was doing."

I closed my eyes. The Rock Meister. *Butt blisters!* "Good. That's good," I said, instead of what I was actually thinking. "Wait, she left an hour ago? I wasn't down here that long." I frowned. "Or was I? How long have I been missing?"

They shared a look that told me I didn't want to know. "What's been going on while I've been down here?" I reluctantly asked.

Another head popped into the circle, shoving Rustin and Lea aside. "Hi, Naida. It's me, London."

"Hi, London," I said, actually smiling. "I'm surprised you're still with us."

He frowned. "What? You're not going to crack a Werewolf in London joke?" The frown turned to a grin.

"Later. I promise."

His grin widened. "I'll hold you to that. Right now, since they're...you know...naked and can't scamper around the countryside for fear of astonishing the pure of heart and stuff, the other guys sent me to report that the zoo has been cracked. There are wild animals everywhere."

My nascent smile died a horrible death.

"And the Enchanted airport just cracked a few minutes ago. I guess there's a plane and a hangar nestled in the breach. Quite literally."

Goddess help me. I couldn't even respond. I was suddenly so weary, I didn't think I could stay upright.

"Naida?" Grym looked as if he might jump into the hole with us. "Are you going to be okay? You look a little pale."

"She does, doesn't she?" London agreed happily. "She's about the color of werewolf Randy's backside. He's a redhead and those cheeks have NEVER seen the light of day, if you know what I mean."

"What are you talking about?" Rustin asked. "He runs around naked all the time."

"In the moonlight, yeah. Don't get confused by the term, flashing the moon. There's no light at night to flash anything."

Rustin sighed. "We'll divvy up the work load, Naida. Don't hyperventilate. Let's just take it one mess at a time. Okay?"

I nodded, but I wasn't convinced. Despite our best intentions, Enchanted had cracked. And I was zero for one on dealing with my toxic artifact.

Not impressive. Not impressive at all.

16

YOUR TIMING MIGHT BE OFF, DUDE!

I needn't have worried about going back to Croakies and seeing it in a less-than-soothing state. We were waylaid a mile from town, a member of the supernormal unit pulling us over with sirens blaring.

Grym sighed as he pulled to the shoulder. "I was expecting this," he told us. "I'm actually surprised they didn't approach me sooner. They're short on supernormal cops and this mess is going to take a lot of manpower to cover up and repair."

I groaned softly. I hadn't even thought about what the cracking meant to a mostly human population. Grym and his unit could rescue zoo animals and pull small aircraft from holes in the runway, but it was going to be a real trick to explain how massive cracks in the earth just disappeared once we stopped the artifact.

If we stopped the artifact.

In my lap, Wicked started to purr, using his unique magic to soothe my jangled nerves. I dug my fingers into his warm fur and let the positive vibrations slow my pulse.

I mentally kicked myself. I couldn't think that way. I *had* to stop it.

Vel barked enthusiastically at the man who'd climbed out of the fire department SUV behind us. He had fiery red hair and a tall, blocky build, and was dressed in firefighter's gear. Brad Spence was a Phoenix shifter with the fire department who worked closely with Grym's supernormal unit. Grym met him with an outstretched hand. "Spence."

"Detective," Spence responded with his soft Southern drawl. "Quite the mess we've got here, huh?"

Grym shook his head. "That's not an overstatement. How's the team? Anybody hurt?"

Spence settled a warm regard on Lea in the back seat. His golden-brown gaze lit up with interest when he looked at her. The two of them had gone on several dates recently, but I had no idea how they had turned out. Judging by Lea's shy smile, I was going to assume they'd been a success.

Spence returned her smile. "Hiya, Lea. You're okay?"

"Fine, yes. Thanks for asking."

For a second, he looked as if he might say more, but he ultimately settled on a nod. The shifter scanned his gaze around the car and greeted each of us. When he got to London, one fiery red eyebrow spiked.

London waved enthusiastically. "Hey! I'm London."

Spence let that sink in for a beat before shifting a questioning look toward Grym. Being a shifter himself, he could easily read the other man's magical form, and he'd know he was a werewolf.

Grym smiled. "Not a joke."

Spence barked out a laugh. "Hiya, London. Give Lon Chaney Jr. my best."

London's eyes sparkled. "I'd love to. Did you know Lon's real name is Wolf Mann?"

Brad snorted. "Now that *is* a joke."

London shrugged, a tiny smile playing on his wide lips.

Spence turned back to Grym, all humor gone. "We need your help at the zoo. Two elephants escaped. A mother and her calf. They aren't dangerous, but they can do a lot of damage without meaning to. Since you're the strongest one in the unit, we nominated you to gather them up."

Grym nodded. "Do you have any idea where they went?"

Grinning, Spence smacked Grym on the back. "Start at the zoo and follow the enormous footprints." He turned away, striding back toward the red SUV.

"What about you?" Grym asked. "You want to help me shove a mama elephant back into her habitat?"

Spence opened the door and turned back to Grym. "No thanks. I've got my own assignment."

"Let me guess. You're rounding up some dolphins that got into the otter pool?"

Spence laughed. "Close. Two adult orangutans have taken over a playground behind a school. Fun times."

"You want some advice?"

"Not really, but go ahead." Spence frowned, as if expecting to be told he'd have to shoot the primates.

"If they start flinging poo, run."

Spence blew a dismissive raspberry. "Working in the supernormal unit, I'm used to poo flinging."

"Do you need help?" Lea asked. She'd climbed out of the SUV and looked concerned. I didn't blame her, poo flinging aside, large primates were no joke.

Spence eyed her for a beat, probably noting the circles under her eyes and her generally disheveled state. It had been a long, exhausting night in the forest. "Sure, if you're up to it. You look a little worn out."

"I am. But can we make a quick stop at the shop so I can change shoes and grab some water?"

"Of course," Spence gave her a gentle smile. She turned to me. "See you back at Croakies in a couple of hours?"

I nodded. "Be careful." Behind me, Vel barked and I had a thought. "Hey, since you guys are going back there, could you take Vel and Wicked home for me?"

"Sure," Lea said. "I'll leave them at my place, just in case..." Her expression turned doubtful as she realized she didn't want to finish that sentence. She finally settled for, "Hex would probably enjoy the company."

I understood her reluctance. Croakies was likely a mess by that point. She didn't want me melting down at the thought of it. "Thanks."

We transferred the critters and climbed back into Grym's car, pulling back onto the road. Glancing at the rearview mirror, my detective addressed his newest passenger. "Can I drop you somewhere, London?"

"I'll go to the zoo," he said. "It sounds like they could use some help."

Rustin nodded. "Me too."

"Good." Grym glanced my way.

"I'm with you." I said.

"You feel like tracking some giant footprints around town?"

"Sounds like the perfect way to end my day."

Giving me a smile of thanks, he patted my knee. "Elephants on the run it is."

An anteater ambled across the parking lot in front of us as we pulled in. A massive yellow snake hung from a light pole, its muscular form wrapping the pole in a deadly embrace. I shuddered. "This is why I took the elephants," I announced to the car at large. "I don't do snakes."

As we pulled into a parking spot, I frowned over at a sight several rows away that I'd never expected to see. "Is that an albino tiger?"

"Yeah," Rustin agreed. "The zoo acquired it last year. Isn't it gorgeous."

"It would be more attractive if it wasn't draped over a school bus with an entire roasted chicken hanging out of its mouth," Grym said.

A few spaces down, a woman with what looked like a dart gun was stretched over a second bus on her belly. Just as she loosed the barb, the tiger stood up and the orange-flecked dart slammed into the chicken.

"I need to have a gander at this," London said. "That one's already immobile," he yelled across to the shooter as he climbed out of the car.

She extended a finger that was generally not used in polite company.

"Cheeky," he said to Rustin.

Shaking his head, Rustin nodded toward a crowd of people waiting outside the gift shop. "I'm going to find out who's in charge and see how I can help."

Grym held out his hand and Rustin shook it. "Good luck," he told our friend. "Stay safe."

London strolled past me and toward the woman on the bus. I watched with interest as he called out to her, trying to get her attention.

She spoke without taking her eyes off the tiger. "Bugger off, wanker. I'm working here."

A group of watchers in a van down the way cheered as

London started to strip. "Your timing might be off, dude," one of them yelled.

I rolled my eyes. What did London think he was going to do?

"I can help," said London as he stepped out of his pants and reached for his boxers.

"I don't need..." the woman started to say, before glancing angrily in his direction. She jerked as if she'd been hit with one of her own darts, then covered her eyes. "Bollocks! I'll call the police, pervert."

With a jolt, I realized what he was going to do. "Grym," I said. "London's about to reveal more than his butt freckles." Apparently the Brit didn't realize mundanes weren't widely aware of supernormals in Enchanted.

Grym's gaze swung in the same direction as mine. He grunted and then sighed. "London, can I speak with you please?"

"It's okay, mate. I got this." His boxers hit the parking lot, setting off a riot of wolf whistles...pun decidedly *not* intended... across the parking lot. Three guys in a truck, wearing oil-stained ball caps, wife-beater tee-shirts, and work jeans were clearly entertained by London's antics.

"London!" Grym barked, "You can't do that here."

The Brit ignored Grym and his form started to shimmer.

"*Slavering centipedes!*" I sent my keeper magic into the air and flung up a hand as the selected artifact sailed my way. It hit my palm and I staggered. Stumbling under the clunky form of the magical vacuum cleaner, I nearly hit the crumbling blacktop before getting both hands on the artifact and grappling for the power button.

"This is no time to clean, lady," said another of the snarky watchers, spurring his friends to laughter.

I glared over at them and settled the cleaner to the

ground, releasing the hose attachment from the base. "Do you want to be the first person I vacuum up?" I'd meant the taunt to be slightly threatening, but the men laughed and waggled their brows, assuming there was some kind of raunchy innuendo in my taunt.

My cheeks were flaming as I turned away.

Grym had reached London at that point and the two were having a low-voiced argument. It appeared that Grym had things well in hand as London reached for his clothes. I started to snap the hose back into place.

With a roar that turned me to jelly, the tiger leaped off the bus, landing lightly on the ground mere feet away from London and Grym.

The Brit gave a sharp-edged yelp and turned into his funky wolfman form in a flash of purple light. As the tiger sprang, massive fangs dripping with spittle, Grym was forced to shift too. I cried out in panic as the tiger slammed into Grym and sent him to his back on the blacktop, claws and fangs flashing. It happened so quickly, I wasn't sure if my gargoyle had completed his shift in time.

"Ah!!!" the three men in the truck yelled. "Did you see that? That weird naked guy turned into Lon Chaney Jr. right in front of us."

"What about the Hulk?" the other one said. "Awesome!"

On his back and struggling to keep the tiger from ripping out his throat, Grym threw me a glare and I shook myself out of my panic attack long enough to hit the power button and point the hose of the cleaner toward the guys in the truck.

A cloud of fine dust spewed from the end of the vacuum and crossed the distance between me and the three hecklers.

As the dust found them, it thickened and formed a wall

of magic that turned them to dull-eyed statues. When they came to in a few minutes, they wouldn't remember anything they'd seen before their dosing.

I turned to the sniper on the bus and found her staring suspiciously at me. When she saw me lift the hose, she raised her hands defensively. "Don't shoot. I'm a witch."

I nodded. Glancing around the parking lot and finding no other observers to be neutralized, I turned off the cleaner.

By the time I'd set the trio of men in memory-loss concrete, Grym had managed to get to his feet and London had hold of the tiger's tail. Snarling and snapping at each other, London and the tiger were running in circles, mutually unhappy.

"Can you please dart the tiger before it eats my friends," I asked the witch.

"I'm trying, aren't I? Those blokes are in my way."

"Guys, can you keep the tiger still so the witch can dart it?" I called out to Grym and London.

Once again on his back, Grym was struggling to evade the oversized fangs. He turned to me with a glower. Still attached to the tail, London snarled.

"Maybe you can just poke it into him," I suggested.

The woman rolled her eyes. "If they'd get out of my way, I could do my job."

"London, let go of the tail and get out of the lady's way."

London leaped onto the tiger's back and sank his fangs into its shoulder.

I dropped my face into my hands. "Idiot."

The tiger reared back and roared, the sound rattling the windows of the car next to me. Then it whipped around and sank its teeth into London's thigh.

London gave a high-pitched yelp and tried to extricate

himself. But the tiger had a solid grip and was rising to its paws.

Grym didn't get up right away, and I was afraid he'd been injured. He looked stunned.

"Grym?"

"I'm...allrigh...t," he finished, his voice sounding slurred.

London yelped again as the tiger's teeth found his backside. It lifted him off the ground and shook him like a rag doll.

I yelled at the witch to shoot the tiger, already, and hurried over to Grym. He shook his head, shoving air with his palms as if to keep me away. "S'kay..." he wobbled as if he might fall over, "Poison...BIG spider. Jusss give me a minute."

"Grym, you need help. Did the tiger bite you?"

Atop the school bus, the witch gave a blood-curdling scream and levitated off the bus. "Spider? I hate spiders!" The woman landed hard in the parking lot and didn't slow down until she'd put half of the lot behind her.

"Seriously?" I yelled after her. Grym managed to get to his feet. Something twitched on the blacktop and I glanced down, seeing nothing at first. Then the pavement moved and I jolted backward with a little girly scream.

A huge, hairy spider that perfectly matched the asphalt skittered past Grym. He lifted a foot and stomped it.

"Ugh!" I said. "That's what bit you?"

He nodded, the action nearly taking him down again. "Rock spiders aren't dangerous to most people, but they're highly toxic to gargoyles."

"Really?" I'd always thought his rocky form was impervious to poisons.

"Really." His head came up when London screamed. He stumbled sideways a few steps from the movement. "We need to..." He took a step and nearly fell over. Holding his head, he wobbled like one of those weighted toys kids liked to punch.

"Oh for..." I marched over to the spot on the pavement where the witch had dropped the gun, and picked up the weapon. Riding a wave of disgust and adrenaline, I strode over and fired the dart into the tiger's backside.

It snarled and tried to whip its head toward me, but London had a grip on its throat and it couldn't reach me. I was over it at that point. "Stop your caterwauling. (No pun intended. Really.) I thought cats *liked* to nap."

The tiger wobbled and snarled, but the snarl was less potent with the dart on board. A few minutes later, the big cat was snoring.

London extricated his bloody and bitten self from the sleeping kitty. He shifted quickly, shuddering as he looked down at the beast. "I hate cats."

I snorted. I couldn't help myself. "Do you need medical help?"

He shook his head, but I noticed he was rubbing his backside. His naked backside. "The shift healed everything up." I averted my gaze because the shift hadn't put his clothes back on. "How come you were naked this time?" As he moved toward the discarded clothing, I put my hands on either side of my face like blinders. Still, my cheeks heated.

"I removed them before I shifted. When you found me in the crack, I'd been scared into a shift when the crevice opened up and swallowed me."

"Yeah, there was a lot of that going on," I said.

I glanced at Grym. "Come on, Rocky. I'll take you to the hospital."

He shook his head. "Just give me a minute. I'll be fine. We still have animals to round up."

17

9-1-1. WHAT'S YOUR EMERGENCY?

A distant explosion shook the ground beneath my feet and I looked up as a cloud of flames and smoke rolled over the horizon. "What do you think that was?" I asked, my pulse spiking.

Grym sighed wearily. "I'll find out." He punched a number into his phone and I heard a woman's voice say, "9-1-1. What's your emergency?"

"Hey, Gladyce, it's Detective Grym. Have you received a report on an explosion northwest of town?"

"Detective Grym, we're just receiving that now. It seems a fissure has opened up at the gas station on Third and High. Fissure ran through an underground tank and sparks set it off."

"Do you need help?"

"First responders are rolling. We'll keep you apprised."

"Thanks, Gladyce. Things are a little crazy today, huh?"

"Yes, sir. But it makes the shift fly by."

"I'll bet." He disconnected and looked my way. "You heard that?"

"I did." The news had taken a little more of the starch out of my shoulders, and my chin was drooping. I'd already felt guilty about not stopping the toxic artifact more quickly. Every disaster that occurred from it just made me feel less adequate.

Grym put an arm around my shoulders and gave me a quick hug. "This isn't your fault. We'll get it under control."

I bit down on an argument for it *all* being my fault, knowing he wouldn't understand. And maybe he'd be right. But I couldn't shake the feeling that magical artifacts were supposed to be my bailiwick. Even toxic ones. And I'd been woefully lacking in dealing with the current one.

We reached a well-traveled area and Grym held up a hand to stop me as he tried to find the trail we'd been following. My phone rang as he was pushing vegetation away and examining small branches for breakage.

I answered without looking at who was calling me. "Hello."

"Naida keeper," said a cool, familiar voice. "I'm calling to see how things are going with your toxic artifact."

My head shot up and panic flared. "Madeline." My thoughts spun as I tried to figure out what to tell her. I finally decided there was no point lying or soft-selling it. She'd find out anyway. "Not good, I'm afraid. Things have gone from bad to worse and much of Enchanted is now being corrupted by it."

Silence met my admission. Was that a judgmental silence? I could feel my shoulders rounding and my posture slumping.

A sigh sifted through the connection. "I'm afraid that's the general state of things. None of the five toxic artifacts is under control. We can't even figure out how to slow them down."

Grym pointed to the ground and took off in a different direction. I followed more slowly, recognizing that we were heading the right way when I spotted several broken branches and a couple of saplings that had been crushed on the ground.

Madeline's tone was heavy. She sounded depressed. I'd never heard her sound like that before. It was...disturbing... to realize there were no experts who could help. The Universal Council and the PTBs were apparently just as much at a loss as I was. I wished that made me feel better. But it didn't.

"If things improve or...there's any change in the situation, please call me."

I blinked in surprise. Maddie generally discouraged contact. She was a busy and powerful witch and had seemingly little time to deal with small cogs like me. "Sure. I'll let you know."

"Thanks." She disconnected without any further niceties.

"Problem?" Grym asked.

I glanced at him. "I'm not sure. That was Maddie."

"She's okay?"

"I don't know."

He stopped and turned to me. "You don't know? What does that mean?"

"It means she sounded despondent. I've never heard her sound that way before. It was unsettling."

"I can imagine." He tugged me close and kissed me on the temple, leaving behind a warm, tingly spot when he pulled away. "Come on. We're getting close. They're heading toward the river."

The bellow of a really large animal gave me a jolt. "That sounded like an elephant," I said, fear prickling my skin.

He grabbed my hand. "Come on!"

We took off running just as an even more desperate bellow sounded. I dug in and ran faster.

The path descended steeply as we neared running water. Tree limbs slashed at my hair and snagged my clothes as I ran after Grym. For a big guy who weighed considerably more than I did, even in his human form, he was fast. I quickly found myself falling behind. When Grym descended quickly on the other side of a rocky rise, I lost him completely.

By the time I topped the rise myself a minute later, my heart was pounding hard enough to make me see stars. I jolted to a stop at the scene before me.

Grym was near the river, facing a frantic elephant with his hands up, palms forward. He held the coiled rope the zoo had given us in one hand and he seemed to be trying to calm the mother elephant. He wasn't having any success. She trotted toward him, her eyes filled with menace and her trunk aggressively swinging.

"Grym?" I said just loud enough that he could hear me.

"The baby went into the river," he said in soft tones. "The current took her downstream. The mother's frantic."

"At least she hasn't gone into the water too," I said, moving slowly closer.

"She was heading in when I came over the rise. She seems to think I'm more of a danger than the current right now."

A tiny trumpeting sound sifted toward us from downstream and the mother trumpeted back, swinging her trunk and backing toward the water.

"We need to stop her and get to the baby," I said.

"I can't get this rope around her neck. She's too agitated." Grym moved closer to the elephant, but there was nothing he could do. Even if he was in his gargoyle form, he wasn't strong enough to wrestle a distressed adult elephant. "It's okay, mama," he soothed, hands still up to ward off her antagonistic movements. "Let us help your baby, okay?"

I considered our options, wishing we'd thought to bring the dart lady. "You don't have any darts in your pockets do you?"

"I have chewing gum in my pocket," he told me. "And the once-laundered tickets from the movie I took you to last week. Nothing helpful."

I bit back an exclamation that neither of us had come prepared. I'd always thought elephants were tame and sweet natured. It had never occurred to me that the pair wouldn't just follow us back. "I can call a magic rope artifact," I told him.

"What does it do?"

"Makes the receiver sleepy," I said.

"That'll work. If we can sedate mama, we can rescue the calf and bring it back here. Then this rope should be enough to encourage mama to follow quietly."

I threw up a hand and called the rope with my keeper magic. A moment later, I heard the tell-tale whisper of sound as it whisked its way through the air and smacked into my upraised palm. Then I stood looking from the rope to the mother elephant.

Another frightened sound from the baby had the mother bellowing and swaying back and forth, her back feet already in the water at the edge of the river. "She's gonna blow," I said helpfully.

"Did you get the rope?" Grym didn't turn to me. He seemed afraid he'd lose the little bit of control he'd gained over the animal if he looked away.

"Yeah. But now that I have it, I don't know how we're

going to get it on mama."

He cursed softly. After a beat, he said, "Walk very slowly down to me."

I did as requested, holding the rope out to him as I approached.

The elephant trumpeted and charged. I yelped and dropped the rope.

In a flash of silver light, Grym transformed into his gargoyle to take the force of her attack. He dove in front of her.

She lowered her head and slammed into him, sending him flying into a nearby tree.

I backpedaled as she swung her head, her angry gaze sliding past me before returning to Grym.

"Are you okay?" I yelled as he groaned and carefully gathered himself to stand.

"I've been better." His voice was the deep, gravely sound of his gargoyle. "Stay back, Naida. She's dangerous."

My gaze swung to the dropped rope and then to the elephant. I had to help or Grym was going to get killed and the baby might die.

"Easy, mama," I said, slowly moving toward the distraught elephant. "We just want to help."

She blew air through her trunk, the sound like an explosion against the backdrop of the raging river.

I closed my eyes and gave myself up to stillness. "Easy," I said again. I adopted a lyrical tone to hopefully calm her. "We're going to help your baby. Wouldn't that be good?" I realized she didn't understand my words. But maybe she'd react to the calm and sing-songy voice. "We want to help you. Help your calf. Get you both home and safe."

Mama blew air again, but her head-swinging had slowed a bit.

"We need to get that rope over her before the baby cries again," I told Grym in the same sing-songy voice.

"Stay back, Naida," he warned again. "I don't want you hurt."

I smiled at the elephant as I slowly eased my hand toward the rope. "She's not going to hurt me. Are you, mama?" I sang. My fingers closed around the rope.

Mama backed another step, her massive feet sinking into the silty bottom. The sensation alarmed her enough to make her jolt and charge forward.

Heading directly for me.

I froze, too scared to move as she lumbered toward me, faster than I expected something so ungainly to move.

She was mere feet away when Grym yelled. "Naida! Throw it!"

My gaze jerked toward his voice, finding him leaping from a high branch of the tree clinging to the edge of the river.

Without thinking, I threw the rope toward his outstretched hand and he caught it.

Mama slammed to a stop when she spotted him, the greater danger in her mind, and she spun, whipping her muscular tail around and hitting me like a fist to the ribs. I went down hard, agony slicing through me, and wheezed in a tortured breath as the massive flat feet of the adult danced all around me, barely missing me several times as Grym fought to subdue her from her back.

It only took seconds for the magical rope to begin working. But they were the longest seconds of my life. I tried to move out of the way, but it was like a hot blade being inserted between my ribs every time I moved.

The elephant finally stopped moving and dropped her head. Grym tied a knot to keep the rope around her thick neck and slid off her back, running over to me. "Naida, honey. Where are you hurt?"

"My ribs. I don't think I can move."

He sighed as the baby trumpeted again. Rubbing a hand over his face, he pulled out his phone. "Hey. Naida's hurt," he said to the person on the other end of the line. "She needs healing and I have to save a baby elephant from drowning in the river. We need you here."

He nodded once and disconnected.

"I know you didn't just call the sprite," I told him in a strained voice. I was afraid to take normal breaths because of the pain. "She wouldn't have just agreed to come without arguing."

He dropped down next to me. "She's not as selfish as you think she is."

"Uh huh," I said in a dry tone. "You *have* met her, right?"

He didn't laugh as I'd hoped. He was so tense I thought his rocky self might splinter and crack.

I reached out and grasped his hand. "Go. Save the baby. I'll be okay."

"I can't leave you."

"You can. I'll be devastated if that baby dies and it's my fault because I kept you here."

He glanced down river, his jaw tight even in his gargoyle form.

"Go. Please."

"Are you sure?"

"Yep. I'm going to just lie here and enjoy the respite. It's been quite the frog-flippin' day."

That time he did laugh. Leaning close, he gave me a warm, quick kiss. "Yell if you get into any trouble."

"I will. Promise."

He took off running. Agony speared my middle, and I fought to keep from yelling for him to come back.

I was pretty sure I was going to die. And I didn't want to die alone.

18

BLAST YE'RE BARNACLED BOTTOM YE SCURVY-RIDDEN SON OF A BLEEPIN' BLACKGUARD!

I lay there trying not to breathe and listening to the roar of the river. The baby elephant hadn't trumpeted for a while, and I tried to tell myself that didn't mean anything dire.

But myself didn't believe it.

The mother hadn't moved at all since Grym tied the magical rope around her neck. Her head hung low and her eyes were closed, her trunk drooping to the patchy grass. I suffered pangs of guilt every time I looked at her. I told myself that sedating her had been the right thing to do. But I couldn't help wondering if she was inwardly stressed but unable to do anything about it because of the rope.

Not for the first time, I decided I needed to do a better job of documenting the artifacts at Croakies so I knew more about what they did. It was a daunting prospect, given that I had thousands of magical items stored in the artifact library. But it needed to be done. Sebille and I were so busy dealing with the everyday stuff, even our best intentions hadn't gotten that research and documentation done.

Maybe I could hire someone for that specific task.

I was so deep into my thoughts that I didn't hear anything until it was nearly on top of me. A distinctive buzzing had me reacting without thinking as a large bug with dragonfly wings flew into my face. I yelped and swung my hand, barely clipping the thing's wings as it dodged out of the way.

"Hey!" the bug objected. "Watch those hands, derf."

I sighed, noting the odd mix of bright colors and patterns covering the bug's bony form as I realized it wasn't a bug. "Finally," I groused. "I thought you'd never get here."

Even as tiny as her face was, Sebille managed to exaggerate her eyeroll to properly illustrate her disdain for me. "I'm sorry, princess. I was kind of busy, you know."

I took a deep breath and expelled it. "Sorry. My ribs hurt and it's making me cranky."

Sebille buzzed away and I jerked, afraid she was leaving in a fit of pique.

The razor edge of agony sliced across my chest at the movement. "Ah!"

But the sprite had just buzzed over to hover in front of the elephant's huge face. I caught myself wondering if elephants ate bugs, and then had to assure myself that I wasn't hoping they did.

"Is that the magical sleep rope from India?"

"Yes," I said, my voice sounding strained. "It's coming in handy."

Sebille buzzed to and fro, her movements dizzyingly fast in her fairy form. "Where's the big hunk of rock?"

"He's saving the baby elephant. And don't call him that. It's demeaning."

She buzzed over and transformed to full size in a burst of silvery light. "Right. And I'm never demeaning."

"Yes," I agreed. "You always are. But this is the very

handsome man I love who also happens to be a cop. So, I'm objecting."

She knelt beside me and laid her hands over my ribs. As sparkly light flared from her hands, a delicious healing warmth infused my ribs. I felt some of the tension leaving my body as she healed me.

"Let me see if I get this so I'm sure not to offend your delicate sensibilities again. If it's someone you don't like it's okay to demean them."

"No...I..."

"If they're ugly, I can demean them?"

"Of course not. I didn't..."

Okay, then, if they're not a cop I can demean them?"

I expelled an exasperated sigh. "Just don't demean anybody. Then we'll be good."

"That's an unreasonable request."

"It's not a request, Sebille. It's an order."

"You're not the boss of me."

"Yes. I am quite literally the boss of you."

"Whatever." She stood up and offered me a hand. "Stop laying around in the dirt. It's unseemly."

I growled and took her hand, letting her pull me up. Brushing dirt off my backside, I asked, "How are things at Croakies? Is Slimy okay?"

She frowned and I braced for bad news. Unfortunately, there was no way to brace for what she told me.

"The fat green squish isn't eating his crickets or pestering me with dictionary tidbits."

My pulse spiked. "That's not good."

"No." Her frown deepened. Crossing her arms over her flat chest, she chewed the inside of her lip. "I'm worried about him, Naida. I even called my mother over for a consult."

Like her daughter, Queen Sindra was an earth fairy, knowledgeable of all things green and growing. But apparently not frogs. "She had no idea how to fix him?"

"She doesn't even know what to fix. She's never seen anything like this." Sebille swung an arm around as if to include all of Enchanted City. She looked ready to cry.

"What? Tell me, Sebille. You're freaking me out here."

"He's..." She swallowed hard. "He's cracking."

I blinked, my brain unable to wrap around what she was telling me. Then it hit me and I felt as if my chest had exploded. All of my organs rebelled at the same time. I wheezed in a tortured breath, doubling over and fighting to breathe while my heart appeared to have stopped and my lungs ceased working.

"Naida?" True to her nature, Sebille sounded more impatient than worried. I knew her well, though, and realized that was how she processed her worry.

"I have to go home."

Sebille shook her head. "The only thing we can do for him is to stop this toxic artifact. And we need to act fast because the cracking is branching out. Lea's shop is cracked now, and the other shops on our street. The destruction is speeding up."

I started pacing, wringing my hands. It wouldn't help, but I had to do something. If I didn't move, I'd lose my mind. "I spoke to Maddie. She said nobody knows how to stop these things. If the best brains in the magical world can't fix this, how in the goddess's bristly arm hairs am I going to?"

"I don't know," Sebille said, tears in her voice. "But we have to. And we have to do it fast."

A small but mighty call came from the woods behind me. I turned to find Grym, soaked and grimy, leading the baby elephant toward us with the non-magical rope.

The baby gave a happy little cry when it saw mama and just about trampled us getting to her.

Grym took one look at our faces and asked, "What's wrong? Is it the squish?"

I sucked in a shaky breath. "Slimy's cracking," I said, the words thick with tears. "We need to figure out how to fix this, fast."

He stared at me for a long moment, emotions flaring in his expressive gaze. After a moment, he nodded, handing me the end of the rope. "Let's get these animals back to the zoo. Then we'll go do that."

Yeah. We'd just go figure it out. Right.

I stood at the end of Arcane Avenue and stared down the street, my heart ripping into pieces at the sight. The road itself was impassable. The asphalt had heaved in sharp, broken chunks against the curb.

Glass littered the sidewalks and most of the windows appeared to be broken. Doors hung at odd angles from their hinges, and cars up and down the street were cattywampus, their dented frames sitting half inside the web of deep crevices the growing artifact had left behind.

Partway down the street, a fountain of water from a broken hydrant spewed into the sky, creating a drain path that followed the natural slant of the street and into the adjoining neighborhood. The firetruck was parked at the entrance to Arcane Avenue, unable to bring their trucks into the devastated area.

A few shop keepers stood on the broken sidewalks, staring morosely at the wreckage the toxic magic had wrought.

"Jeezopete," I breathed as I stared at the sight. "This is horrible." Tears burned my eyes. How was I going to fix the damage and subdue the magic?

Grym squeezed my shoulder. "You'll figure this out, Naida. I have faith in you."

I shook my head, not believing him. "Let's go check on Croakies." I stepped over a chunk of metal that looked to have once been a car's bumper and picked my way carefully toward the store.

As I stepped into Croakies, the floor vibrated gently beneath my feet. I stopped abruptly and crouched there, placing my hand flat on the debris-strewn carpet. The carpet warmed beneath my palm and, remembering the alien moss, I jerked my hand away. Did the vibrations and heat mean the crack was growing again? It seemed likely.

"What is it?" Grym asked.

"I don't know," I told him. "A vibration. I have no idea what it means." Just one more thing I didn't understand. I added it to the collection of unknowns that was already insurmountable and slid my gaze toward Slimy's tank.

A sharp scream escaped and my hand flew up to cover my mouth. Slimy's glass tank was on the ground, over-turned, and the glass was shattered. His warming light and the rock he liked to lay on were both missing. Likely buried beneath the wreckage of the tank. I had to step over an eight-inch-wide branch of the fissure to reach the destruc-tion. My throat clogged with fear, I carefully moved the remains of the tank, looking for my fallen frog.

"He's not there," Sebille said, her tone suspiciously gentle.

I glanced up at her. "Where..." I had to swallow to finish the question. "Where is he?"

Sebille motioned for me to follow her. We picked our

way over fallen shelves, and books lying in ungainly piles. Some of the tomes had been stacked neatly against the wall. It looked as if Sebille had attempted to put the mess into some kind of order. Unfortunately, the bookshelves were broken and twisted and we wouldn't be able to reshelve the books until they were fixed.

I didn't even want to see what the artifact library looked like.

I couldn't have imagined it if I'd tried. But it wasn't at all what I'd expected.

"Watch out," Sebille said mildly.

I gave a soft yelp and ducked as Shakespeare's desk shot past me, nearly taking off the top of my head. I stumbled backward as a magical dancing hat and its feather followed along behind the desk, giving me a jaunty salute of its brim as it passed.

His gaze stuck on the flying artifacts just as mine was, Grym bumped into me and had to grab my arms so I wouldn't fall. "What's going on?"

I stood with my mouth hanging open. All of the artifact shelves—dozens of floor-to-ceiling metal units that had been thirty feet high and covered with artifacts—were bent and bowed, their shelves naked and dust-covered. The units' feet had been captured, consumed, and twisted inside a seemingly endless array of secondary crevices branching away from the main one.

And the artifacts...

I shook my head, glancing at the sprite. "How did you do this?" *This* included thousands of floating and flying artifacts, hanging above the floor and the crevice, so they wouldn't be damaged by the toxic magic.

"I asked mother to bring the fae and help. It took every bit of the magic we all had, combined, to manage it."

I could believe it. "You saved them."

Sebille frowned. "Not yet. But hopefully they'll stay safe until we find a fix."

I realized what she was saying. If the cracking continued as it had been, the toxic magic might very well break down Croakies' walls and roof and expose the artifacts to the world. A world filled with unscrupulous supernormals and ignorant mundanes.

A new determination found me. I needed to stop the artifact.

I looked at Sebille. "Slimy?"

A flushing sound had me calling for a weapon and I reached up to catch Blackbeard's sword. I nearly missed its arrival given that it had been floating by much nearer than I'd expected. A heartbeat later, a messy collection of ragged feathers and tatty claws smacked into my chest with an alarmed, "Bwawk!"

"Blast ye're barnacled bottom ye scurvy-ridden son of a bleepin' blackguard! I'll see ye're bones carved into utensils for the devil's tea!" As SB untangled his long-dead limbs and painfully attached his talons to my shoulder, his eyes went wide. "Ah, lass. My apologies. I thought ye were the black-guard what cursed the hold of this here ship."

Wincing, I tried to pry his talons from my flesh, only managing to loosen them slightly as he flapped his wings with affront. But there wasn't time to respond as a large form shoved its bulk through the dividing door into the library.

"It's about time," the creature said. "I've been waitin' on those ingredients to seal this fissure. This is no time to be gettin' a mani-pedi, Naida keeper. Why does the king believe you're a reliable ally? I've gotten more reliability from my ancient rock saw and that's not sayin' much."

The Rock Meister.

I bit back a groan, telling myself that the foul creature might mean the difference between beating the toxic magic or not beating it.

I grimaced as the thought stirred that the latter was the more likely scenario. "Aelice," I said in greeting. "It looks like you haven't had much luck fixing the crack." I knew as soon as I said it, that it was a mistake. The ogre stiffened and stood taller, the course orange hair on her body bristling like a dog's ruff. "Aelice *the Amiable,*" she responded, her tone stiff. "And, no, Naida keeper. As you can see..." She swept an arm around the room. "I've made no progress, because I haven't received any of the items I requested."

"Right. Sorry. Lea has the moss. She was called away on a crack-related emergency and Hobs..." I frowned. Why hadn't Hobs and Baca returned with the filigreed rock? I realized I hadn't noticed where they'd gone when we'd left the springs. I glanced at Grym.

He nodded. "I'll find them." He gave me a sweet kiss. "I'll see you later, huh?"

"Yes. Thank you." Turning to the Meister, I said, "ATA, you'll have your ingredients soon. Now, if you'll excuse me, I have a friend to tend."

The Meister snorted unattractively. "The frog? Why would you waste time on that fat green slug? He's worthless."

I bit back the response I wanted to make and stepped around her, heading upstairs before I said something I'd regret.

19

YOU MIGHT HAVE A FEW CRICKETS INSIDE YOUR DISHWASHER

S till panting from having had to basically scale the stairs to the second level, I skidded to a stop in the doorway of my apartment, my mouth dropping open. "Wow. Did the artifact do this?"

Though the place looked like it had undergone an earthquake, I saw no visible fissures in the space.

Sebille sighed. "No. It was hurricane Aelice."

"Ugh!" I said, picking up a giant pair of lace panties with two fingernails and grimacing. "This is disgusting."

"I know, right? Who would have guessed *that* shrew would wear lace panties?" Sebille kicked a small pile of clothing aside and headed for the kitchen. Though the apartment was basically a studio, there was a small area set off to the side where there were appliances, cabinets, and a sink. There was one small window over the sink. It provided descent sunshine, making the place feel warm and cozy instead of just small. The window overlooked the street below, and the shops across from Croakies.

The sink was overflowing with dirty dishes and discarded foam take-out containers. Large, greasy fingerprints coated every surface, including a peanut butter jar sitting on the counter, which contained nothing but a jelly-coated knife.

Sighing, I realized I'd need to go grocery shopping when things returned to normal. *If* things returned to normal.

Sebille opened the dishwasher and pulled out the bowl I used for popcorn. Slimy's heat lamp sat on the upper rack, bathing the lower rack with warmth. I frowned. "You put him in the dishwasher?"

"Think about it, Naida," the sprite said as she set the bowl on the counter. "What part of this apartment was this slob least likely to get into?"

Eyeing the sink full of dishes, I had to concede the point. "Okay. You're right." I stared at the glass bowl, the glass was thick and pebbled, making it impossible to see inside without walking closer. I suddenly feared seeing what condition my friend was in, and my heart started to pound.

Sebille glowered at me, her bony arms crossed over her flat chest. I knew what she was thinking, she'd cared for the little guy all day while I'd been doing other things. If she could do that, I could spend time and care on him too.

I nodded, my feet fighting me as I tried to step closer.

"I'll get him some crickets," she told me, "I couldn't leave them up here because they made too much noise and the ogre princess threatened to dump them out the window." I watched her head back downstairs, putting off walking over to the bowl for as long as I could.

Only the knowledge that Sebille would be back soon and she'd glower at me some more if I didn't man up made me walk over and look down into the bowl.

It was both better and worse than I'd expected.

Better because Slimy hadn't been cleaved into pieces by the dreaded cracking magic. The fissures were shallow and dry. Worse because there were a lot of them, and because he looked like he was barely clinging to life. "Oh, buddy." Tears slid down my cheeks, some of them landing on the puff of soft green moss draping his squishy form.

I touched the moss with a fingertip and found it moist and cool. I hoped it was something the fairies had cultivated in the giant greenhouse behind Lea's shop and that the fairy magic was soothing him.

As I tucked the moss more closely around him, Slimy's eyes slitted open and his throat pulsed a few times.

Hey, Naida, he said, his voice weak and rusty inside my mind.

"Hey, squish. You're looking very svelte. Have you been eating your bugs?"

He shifted beneath the moss, his eyes seemingly having trouble staying open. *Yeah, about that. You might have a few crickets inside your dishwasher.*

Grimacing, I narrowed my eyes at him. "You were playing with your food again and it got away from you?"

Something like that.

His bulgy eyes closed on a shaky sigh. Tears burned my eyes at seeing him looking so pathetic. Though my first experience with the frog had been...challenging...I'd grown to love him and the eclectic range of knowledge he sought out and shared on a regular basis.

Even when he presented it in a snotty tone of voice.

I plucked out his small pool and filled it with fresh, warm water. "Have you had your medicine today?"

The little green man coughed wetly, his entire body shuddering under the assault. Panic sliced a path through my chest.

Sebille forced it on me. But it won't do any good, since it's the toxic magic that's causing my problems.

"I explained that to you, squish," Sebille said as she came into the room carrying a container with air holes and part of an egg carton inside. "It's not cough syrup. Lea put together a mix of immunity vitamins and proteins to keep you strong until we can stop the toxic magic."

Whatever. His body twitched in what I assumed had been meant to be a shrug. Frogs don't have shoulders, so it's hard for them to perform that particular maneuver.

I glanced at Sebille and she looked grave. It was unusual for the frog not to argue with the sprite. They both seemed to enjoy the mental and verbal exercise.

Sebille handed me the container holding Slimy's live crickets and turned away. A moment later, a suspicious sniff sounded from her direction.

I dumped a couple of the crickets into Slimy's bowl, but he didn't even look at them. Then I covered the bowl with the splatter guard from my frying pan to keep the crickets inside. Slimy became so still and quiet that I feared he'd fallen back to sleep.

Closing the container back up, I put it on the counter. Blast the Meister to Hades and back. She could just deal with the noise.

My chest hurt. And my hands. I looked down at them and realized I'd stopped breathing and had formed my hands into tight fists. Rage spiked through me, and I ground my teeth against it.

Why had the stupid artifact landed in Croakies? Why was it ripping my city apart? And why had it made my friend sick?

Sebille came back with another, smaller bowl. She avoided my gaze, and I knew if our gazes caught, we'd be wearing the same expression. "This has a tincture to help with the cracking of his skin."

I nodded and carefully removed the moss from Slimy, picking him up and gently settling him into the warm, muddy-looking water.

I covered the bowl again and Sebille set his warming lamp above it. Then, we both just stood there, as if we hadn't a clue what to do with ourselves. There were many things we should have been doing. Too many things. But I felt unable to move away from that bowl, with its squishy green passenger.

When Slimy's voice entered my mind, I twitched in surprise. I'd thought he was asleep.

You need to find the common weakness between all five toxic strains.

Sebille and I shared a confused glance.

"Huh?" I said.

The five escaped toxic artifacts. He said by way of explanation. *You won't be able to defeat them on their own. They're tied together somehow. You'll need to work together and stop them all at the same time. That's the only way.*

"Where did you get that idea?" Sebille snapped.

I knew what she was probably thinking. The last thing we wanted was to take on partial responsibility for four more of the toxic artifacts. We had our hands more than full with the one we had.

I've been meditating. It just came to me.

Knowing there had to be more to it than that, I said, "What is their shared weakness?"

He sighed in my mind. *I don't know. Sorry. I wish I could tell you that.*

I sighed too. "So do I, buddy."

"Hello? Am I the only one who cares about fixing this crack?"

I closed my eyes and dropped my head onto the table.

The Meister.

A plump glower surrounded by frizzy orange hair poked around the doorframe. The creature stepped over the threshold and stood glaring at us, her fuzzy, muscular arms crossed over her chest. "I can't believe you're up here fussing with that frog when the world is cracking apart."

Something had changed with the Meister. At first, I couldn't figure out what it was. She was a bad-tempered creature all the time as far as I could tell. But there was something else. A new glitter to her orange-pupiled eyes.

Tears?

Then it hit me. "Rhorr's kingdom has been struck by the toxic magic, hasn't it?"

She blinked in surprise, sniffled, and then nodded brusquely. "While you stand there communing with a reptile, my people are fighting for their lives."

I closed my eyes, fighting my own fears and frustration.

Amphibian, said a small, tired voice in my head.

"Huh?" Judging by the glower the Meister redirected toward Slimy's spa in a bowl, he'd projected the correction to her as well.

Frogs are from class Amphibia, whereas reptiles are class Reptilia. While both classes are cold blooded, we are not members of the same family.

The ogre looked like she could chew nails. "Who cares?"

Amphibians care. And, I'm guessing reptiles care too.

I fought a smile at the condescending and slightly smug tone of voice. He almost sounded like his old self.

The Meister growled, the sound vibrating on the air between her and the frog. Sebille and I moved to stand between her and the bowl.

"Step down, ogre," Sebille said with her own growl. "Slimy is fighting for his life right now. Just as your people are. While he clearly isn't important to you, he is to us and we won't have you hassling or harming him."

The Meister stilled, jaw tight and fists clenched. "We don't have time for his sermonizing about cold classes," she said. The ogre didn't seem to realize she wasn't making any sense. "My people are losing their homes. Some of them have been caught in the cracks. I need those ingredients so I can stop it."

I frowned, not wanting to be the one to tell her that her fix probably wouldn't help. But if we were going to trust Slimy—and I did—we would need everyone on the same page. "About that..." I said. "Slimy has had a revelation about how to stop the toxic artifact. I believe he may be on to something."

To my surprise, the ogre didn't resist hearing new information. Maybe she hadn't been as sure of her fix as she'd seemed. "Tell me."

"He believes the key is to tackle all five escaped artifacts simultaneously. He thinks there's a commonality between all five that we can use to defeat them."

The ogre seemed to be thinking about that. After a moment, she said, "Go on."

"Right now, magical people around the world are working to defeat five different artifacts. The last time I spoke to a PTB about their efforts, it sounded as if they weren't having any better luck than we are. I'm just postulating here, but maybe Slimy's right. Maybe if we combined our efforts, focusing on a single component that all five are susceptible to, we could finally do what none of us individually can accomplish."

"That makes sense. But what's the common weakness?"

I looked at Sebille. She looked back at me. Neither of us

had a clue. "Figuring that out is the second thing we need to do."

"What's the first?" the Meister asked.

"Getting the other teams on board," I said.

And that wasn't going to be easy.

20

MY JOB SUCKS PUFFER FISH

The bell on the front door jangled unpleasantly. I moved past the Meister and worked my way down the fractured stairs. The damage had grown so bad that the process felt more like I was descending a climbing wall than walking down stairs, and it took several minutes to accomplish.

Long enough that the delegation standing in the book store was looking distinctly sour by the time I entered through the broken dividing door, panting from the effort.

A tall woman with fine dark hair pulled up into a small bun at the back of her head, stood between four...men? Each man was clad in a dark blue uniform, with patches aplenty sewn down the fronts of their jackets in vertical rows. Looking to be around seven feet tall and densely muscled, the men didn't quite look human.

"Bow to Queen Kaith," demanded the man standing at the queen's right hand. He was easily the largest of the four males in her delegation, and his heavy body was nearly square with muscle. He wore his uniform with the confidence of someone who'd worn it a long time and had seen much success using its influence.

The trolls. Awesome.

I wasn't royalty, but Croakies was my kingdom nonetheless. The uniformed troll clearly thought he could come into my kingdom and boss me around. He was wrong. "Queen Kaith," I said instead, giving her a smile. "It's a pleasure to meet you. What brings you to Croakies?"

The woman's dark brown eyes bulged with affront that I hadn't prostrated myself before her. Honestly, they'd bulged before I irritated her, and would continue to bulge after.

Trolls had several distinct features that marked them if one knew what they were looking for. They were excessively tall. They had bulgy eyes and bulbous, veiny noses. They were squarely made, and if you were near enough to look inside their mouths...not recommended...you would discover that they had gobs of tiny, conical teeth that could inject a nerve agent into their enemies, paralyzing them.

"Naida keeper. I was waiting for your visit to my queendom." The queen tilted her head like a particularly ugly bird. "You never came."

I held onto my smile through sheer will power. "As you can imagine, Your Majesty, I've been busy trying to stop what you see around you from happening."

The queen scoffed in a queenly fashion. "It appears you have not been successful."

I didn't quite manage to keep from grimacing at that. Seeing she'd hit her mark, Kaith stepped closer, baring her teeth in a terrifying display of aggression. "My queendom is breaking, Naida keeper. I've been told it is your artifact that is doing it. That is more than an unfortunate occurrence," she said, poking me in the chest with a thick finger. "I am considering it an act of war."

My gaze flew wide. "I have not started a war with the trolls," I told her, panic flaring in my chest. If Queen Kaith thought we were attacking her people, she wouldn't hesitate to retaliate. "As you can see, Your Majesty, my town is also being torn apart. In fact, this problem spans the entire continent."

"Then call in the Universal Council," she demanded, rage sparking in her dark eyes. "Get those worthless busybodies off their backsides and put them to work fixing it." She stepped closer, her breath a sour breeze across my face. The thick finger dug painfully into my breast bone. "If you do not fix this within twenty-four hours, Naida keeper, I will return and I'll have my entire army with me. Blood will flow, Keeper. And I'll start with yours. Do I make myself clear?"

All the color leeched from my face. I felt it fleeing. Swallowing a fist-sized lump in my throat, I nodded. "Perfectly clear." The words had come out sounding strangled.

Queen Kaith spun on her heel and strode to the door, which magically opened before her. She'd stepped through, followed by three of her guards. The fourth guard, the man who'd spoken first, fixed me with a terrifying glower. "Twenty-four hours, Keeper. Or we'll be back."

I concentrated on keeping my knees locked and my lungs filling with air until they were outside, so I didn't fall down and forget to breathe. Then I ran over to lock the door behind them and collapsed against it, letting the tears fall until they'd drained me of the will to move.

$\sim$

"NOBODY HAS TIME FOR THAT," Madeline Quilleran, Power That Be for the North American continent barked testily.

I'd been expecting that response, but it still stung. After

all, I was trying to stop the toxic artifacts before they destroyed the continent. My own doubts made her words sting more. After all, how could I, of all the talented and powerful supernormals involved in trying to stop the artifacts, possibly know anything worthwhile?

In fact, I didn't know anything. All I had were speculations and potentials. Probably the same as everyone.

"I'm only asking for a half hour," I explained, digging in my heels. "We can meet through communication mirrors and compare notes. It might be helpful and I doubt it will cause any delays. We'll all still have people working on the relic problem right? I know I will. But there might be something in the collective consciousness that will help all of us. Maybe even something we knew but hadn't connected to the problem."

Maddie stared at me from the other end of our communication. I could only see her head and the tops of her shoulders, so I speculated she was using a wall mirror to talk to me. I'd been lucky to get her online to start with, given that she was actively involved in trying to stop three of the five toxic artifacts.

Her black hair was lank and untidy, pulled back in a low ponytail that looked as if she'd just grabbed it and stuffed it into a twisty without any thought to how it looked. Her intense, yellow eyes were red-rimmed, and dark circles underscored them. She appeared to be wearing one of her trademark black dresses, but the fabric was wrinkled and covered in something that looked like dust. Maddie's sharply-defined cheekbones looked sharper than usual, the hollows in her cheeks emphasizing her natural bone structure.

Confronted with my determined argument, she closed her eyes and rubbed her hands over her face. Then she sighed. "I'll agree that we're at a loss as to how to stop these artifacts. The entire East coast is on fire. Hundreds of fires and explosions have run millions of people out of the area. Homes and forests destroyed, people burned and succumbing to breathing disorders and worse. I've heard the reports on your area, and it appears the damage has spread into the mountains and is moving outward like a crack in a car's windshield. There's every reason to suppose it will consume the entire middle of the country if you don't find a way to stop it."

I barely bit back a groan. I'd been so focused on fighting the artifact around Enchanted, I hadn't taken the time to find out how far it went. Another wave of self-doubt assailed me and I didn't respond.

"The West coast is flooding. For some inexplicable reason, the ocean is moving inland. Huge chunks of California and Washington State are completely under water and it's rising. Mexico has had hundreds of tornadoes in the last two days. Storms are tearing everything in their path into dust. Canada is under some kind of depressive magic. Suicides have risen a thousand percent, and even the animals are depressed. To make things worse, the dead are walking out of cemeteries and preying on the living. Everything has been poisoned by these toxic artifacts. The continent is under siege."

I sagged under the power of her report, realizing that what I'd been dealing with was nothing compared to the rest of the continent. "I'm so sorry, Maddie. I hadn't realized."

Her eyes glistened with unshed tears, a sight that affected me like nothing else could.

"This is biblical, Naida. It has the potential to send us sliding into the ocean, literally, if we don't stop it soon."

"Then give me this half hour, Maddie. Please. It sounds as if we have nothing to lose by doing it. And potentially something to gain."

The powerful witch stared at me for a long moment, her mouth tightened into a thin line. I'd just about given up when she finally gave me a stiff nod of agreement. "All right, Naida. I'll admit to your point. We have little to lose from trying. It makes sense to combine our knowledge to determine if there might be an answer to the toxic magic there. I'll be in touch once I've notified everyone who would need to be included. Please ensure you invite only those who might reasonably be considered to have something useful to contribute."

I bit back a snide remark and simply nodded. I wasn't there to waste everybody's time. "I will." It occurred to me that I should tell her about Queen Kaith's threats so she'd know how motivated I was, but the devastated look on her face made me keep my mouth shut. She didn't need any more pressure at the moment.

Madeline disconnected without another word, and I sagged with weariness. Whatever we figured out regarding how to fix our problems, I had no doubt the path forward was going to be complex and difficult. The thought made me want to take a nap. Unfortunately, I didn't have time to think about that, because the ground beneath my feet started to shake.

It started with a brief tremble and left me wondering if it had been my imagination. But seconds later, the tremble became a rumble, and was large enough to make the communication mirror bobble on its feet.

I leaped toward the mirror and managed to get a grip on it before it fell. Sending keeper magic into it, I sent it floating with the other artifacts, so it wouldn't fall and break. A long, sharp creaking sound had my gaze lifting toward my apartment, and my horrified gaze locked onto the stairway leading up there. Some volatile energy was twisting the stairway, making it squeal and tear beneath the violence of the power directing it.

My instinct was to back away. To take cover. But then I thought of Slimy and knew I had to get upstairs. Forcing my feet to move, I started walking and then running as the stairs began to splinter and give way to the naked power assailing it. I leaped two steps, knowing I had maybe seconds to get to the top. As my foot landed after another two-step leap, the stair twisted out from under me, and I went down, my knee slamming into the rise of the step above it. Pain sheared through my knee cap and I knew I was going to feel that one for a long time.

I reached for the railing to pull myself upright, but my fingers caught only air. The railing moved away from me as the entire stairway writhed across the broken concrete below.

Another wave of shaking splintered lumber, pulling nails out of the walls, and sending the twisted corpses of the shelving units slamming to the ground. Dust flew and chunks of concrete littered the air, ripping into the floating artifacts like bullets shot from a gun.

The rafters high above my head squealed and warped, more dust and chunks of wood plunging downward to join the tattered artifacts the earthquake had already claimed. I needed to check on the communication mirror, but I couldn't spare a glance.

I was a heartbeat away from joining the broken magic on the floor of the library. Adrenaline surging, I shoved to my feet and leaped up three stairs, my toes barely touching the shifting wood before I was lunging forward again. I hardly noticed the pain of a large splinter stabbing my palm as I hit the landing, which swam through the air like a broken dock in a hurricane.

Throwing myself toward the door, I yanked my foot off the landing just as it plunged downward, crashing into the growing crevice and disappearing in a wash of sawdust, lumber, and twisted metal.

I halted in the doorway just long enough to take stock of my rolling apartment, seeing the pictures that had crashed to the floor, and the dishes the ogre had left on the table, sink, and counter broken and capsized.

Slimy's bowl teetered on the edge of the countertop. I lunged for it, catching it with my fingertips just as it started to fall. Then I scurried toward my bed and jumped into it, pulling the bedding over our heads. If we crashed through the floor, the mattress might save us from serious injury. If the roof crashed down on top of us, hopefully the pillows and covers would mute the damage.

With nothing else to do, I shielded Slimy's bowl with my body, and tried to breathe through the fear.

The roar I hadn't even realized had filled the space began to fade. The shaking eased shortly after that. I was in the fetal position wrapped around Slimy's bowl as the room fell into relative silence, only the occasional creaking of stressed framing intruding on the quiet.

I started to relax, opening my mouth to ask Slimy if he was okay.

With a horrendous cracking sound, the floor beneath my bed gave way and I screamed as we plunged downward. The scream was swallowed by the crashing and squealing of shattering structures and then died when we slammed down so hard the air was punched from my lungs by the concussion.

Silence returned. But there was no comfort in it. I shoved covers back and jumped out of bed, still guarding the squish's bowl. My foot hit a debris-strewn floor and my ankle twisted. I stumbled forward with a cry, dropping Slimy's bowl before throwing out a hand to catch myself on a fallen two-by-four. I screamed again as my hand came down on something pokey that was driven into my palm by the weight of my fall like a hammer.

I kept screaming as agony razored through my hand and ratcheted up my arm. Pulling away from the source of my pain, I screamed harder as the nail that was embedded in my palm slowly slid free.

Tears on my cheeks, I cradled my bleeding hand and bawled like a baby, the fear and frustration of the past day making it hard to get my emotions under control.

Then I remembered Slimy and shoved tears away long enough to look around. My bed had landed on the edge of the fissure, which had widened to the size of a creek, the other side twenty yards away. I started forward, afraid I'd find the frog crumpled in the bottom of the crack. Without warning, my bed broke down the middle and fell into the crack, disappearing from sight.

"No!" I screamed, frantically searching for the bowl. "Slimy!"

"We've got him, Miss."

I whipped around on a cry of surprise and saw Hobs and Baca standing in front of an archway built into the wall. Sure enough, Baca was holding the bowl, though it appeared to be half as big as she was.

"He's okay," the little brownie said.

"Thank the goddess," I exclaimed, expelling a rush of air. "I panicked."

Then I realized they were standing before a broken wall.

Hobs had built his home inside the walls of Croakies. "Your house!" I said. "It's been destroyed." Or had it?

They both shook their heads. Then they stepped aside and I stared at the archway that was the entrance to their hidey hold. I sucked in a gasp of surprise.

"It's not on this plane," Hobs said with a smile. "The cracking can't damage it."

He wasn't kidding. It wasn't even in the same universe with my house. Or, more accurately, my apartment.

The archway framed a door made of crystal. It was open enough for me to see shiny marble floors and elegant furniture. A chandelier sparkled above a large foyer with a wide, curving staircase at its center. Enormous vases of flowers sat on either side of the staircase, their smaller counterparts decorating every visible flat surface. There was a small round table in front of the crystal door, and it held an enormous platter filled with...

My nostrils flared under the rich aroma of moist chocolate goodness and I found myself walking toward the platter with my arms outstretched, my feet shuffling through the debris as if I were a zombie seeking brains. "Are those frosted brownies?"

"Yes, miss."

I probably would have kept shambling toward the gooey goodies if my injured hand hadn't bumped a fallen board, sending agony spiraling through me.

I sucked air.

Hobs shot toward me. "Miss! There's a hole in your hand."

"There is," I said more calmly than I'd thought I could manage." Holding my arm close so I wouldn't bump it again, I kept my gaze averted. It was cowardly, I know. But I couldn't look at the bloody hole.

I didn't even look when the nurse gave me shots or took blood.

"We need to get Sebille," Baca said, her small features going tight with fear.

"I will. Just give me a minute..." My knees suddenly sagged out from under me and I headed for the floor. Sparkling white energy filled the space just behind me and I landed on something mildly comfortable.

A chair.

I glanced at Hobs. "I didn't do it, Miss. You must have called to the artifact without realizing."

I frowned, shifting on the seat as the cushion rolled beneath me. "Maybe." I closed my eyes and sat back.

The seat rolled again and my eyes shot open. Which chair had I called?

The seat pinched my bum.

I shot out of it, whirling as Casanova's chair danced away from my kick and flew across the room.

"Pervert!" I yelled at the retreating chair. *Was that a husky laugh bouncing in its wake?* I looked at Hobs and Baca. "Can you protect Slimy for me? I need to get...fixed."

"Sure, Miss."

I limped away, heading toward the big door at the back of the library. I'd go see if Queen Sindra would heal my nail protrusion.

And maybe my knee.

And my wrist. And ankle.

Sighing, I jolted to a stop, realizing I wasn't going anywhere. I looked out over the massive fissure bisecting my artifact warehouse.

And sagged anew.

My job sucked puffer fish.

21

YOUR…COUNCILNESS

Having received word from Madeline an hour later, I stood in front of the mirror and requested the number she'd given me. Then I waited, expecting to see Felonius again, and the inside of the Quilleran manor.

What I saw had my eyes going round.

As the foggy connection cleared, I found myself staring at the Universal Council, the same dour faces arrayed around the same curved dais as the last time I'd visited the chamber.

Madeline was standing before the council table, her gaze focused on me. "You're late," she informed me, leaving me with pink cheeks and an excuse trying to escape my knotted tongue.

However, she didn't wait for the excuse. Her gaze swept the room, never focusing on the council behind her.

I wondered if they were simply there to observe and wouldn't join in the conversation, which would be all right by me. Council members were generally unpleasant, and most of them had judgmental eyebrows.

"Thank you all for joining in," Maddie began. "I know you're all busy trying to stop the toxic relics. We're gathered here for a *brief*..." she emphasized the word while glaring in my direction as if my fondest hope in life was to draw the event out as long as I could. "...very brief discussion on a potential option for dealing with the pentagram artifacts."

Her reference was one I hadn't heard before. I blinked, the thought crossing my mind that I'd missed something. Had I joined the wrong call?

"One of our artifact keepers has a theory. After listening to her rather lengthy proposal..." she pierced me with a fresh glower. "...I determined it might be worth exploring further." She waved a hand in my direction. "Go ahead, Naida."

Heat burned my face and I was glad I couldn't see the other callers' faces as a frog grabbed my throat and I had to clear it several times before words would come out. "Um. Er...ahem."

"Spit it out Keeper," said a council woman near the end of the dais. My gaze shot to the woman sitting next to her. My mother, whom I'd only recently learned was on the Universal Council.

Narina Griffith, otherwise known as my mother, gave me a faint smile and a small nod of encouragement.

I took a deep breath. "It was recently brought to my attention that the five missing artifacts could potentially have a common weakness. Something we could use to stop them all at the same time."

"Who brought that to your attention?" asked the cranky council woman next to mother.

I opened my mouth and then slammed it shut again. I really didn't want to tell them it was my talking frog.

Yes, council members were magical beings.

Yes, they understood and accepted such things as magical frogs.

But that didn't mean they'd see Slimy as a worthy resource for defeating toxic artifacts.

"Why is that pertinent," my mother asked.

"If we're going to listen to anything this child has to say, we need to understand if her source is qualified."

"That *child*," mother said, "is my daughter. Her word alone gives her source weight." She gave me another nod. "Continue, Naida."

I inclined my head in thanks. "My source has been poisoned by the fissure artifact that's destroying Enchanted and the surrounding area. He is a magical creature that has been integral to many investigations."

Not the least of which was the rune key adventure, wherein we stole a dangerous and highly protected artifact...the artifact of artifacts...from the Universal Council's own vault in an effort to save Queen Sindra and the fae from certain death.

But for obvious reasons, I didn't want to bring that up to them.

"I believe it's the magical talking frog," Maddie said helpfully.

I cringed inwardly.

"Yes," sneered a pinch-faced man with slicked-back black hair and oversized canines. The vampire councilman sat at the other end of the dais. "We're well aware of the frog's ability to stick his snout into places it doesn't belong."

Holy frog flatulence!

I tensed. My little presentation wasn't going well.

The stern-faced man at the center of the dais slammed a gavel and the others fell silent. "If we are to keep this brief as promised, let the girl give her report."

All council faces turned to me.

I cleared my throat. "Yes. Okay. Slimy pointed out that the poisonous artifacts all appeared to have something in common." It suddenly hit me that Maddie had identified that connection by referring to the artifacts as the pentagram relics. "In this case, it appears to be their associations with the five elements, earth, air, fire, water, and spirit. All the components of the perpetual life cycle."

"Yes, girl," said the fish-faced council woman to the leader's right. "We already know that."

"Yes," I said, nodding. "But have you taken that realization to the next step?"

With that question, I'd broken the inquisitor's code. I didn't know the answer to my own question. *Had* they taken it to the next step?

"What next step?" asked the small, blocky man with the pig nose who sat next to the fish.

I had a moment of sheer panic. They wanted me to give them the answer. I didn't have the answer. Did I? The discussion of Slimy had tripped something in my brain that I hadn't been able to identify. Something about the current mess.

Something having to do with...something we'd done before.

"Naida?"

My mother's inquisitive tone jerked me out of my thoughtful daze. Was it possible? I blinked, my thoughts tangling like a nest of snakes. I blinked again. And my brain untangled. I glanced up and said, "The Rune Key."

Chaos exploded in the room.

Having been there before with the same artifact, I crossed my arms over my chest and waited it out. Eventually, they'd get to me. And when that happened, I could plead my case. In the meantime, they wouldn't listen, so there was no point.

"Have you lost your frog flippin' mind?"

I turned to Madeline and sighed. "Probably."

"What is it with you and that artifact? What? You won't rest until it gets into the hands of the wrong supernormal and the world ends?"

Irritated by her hyperbole, I didn't bother trying to mollify. To be honest, I didn't have it in me at that point. "Not the end of the world, no. But I know a few supernormals who could stand a good shaking up."

We glared at each other for several beats. At some point the arguments around the dais stopped and someone called my name.

Madeline's brows lifted.

I shrugged. "What?"

"Naida keeper!"

I jumped, turning to the brown-skinned man at the center of the table. The Head Council. "Yeah?"

He stared at me, clearly appalled by my lack of deference. I would probably be appalled later. At the moment, I just wanted to say my piece and get out of there.

But my mother's glower pierced my devil-may-care attitude and I dug deep to find a respectful attitude. "Your... Councilness."

Maddie grimaced. Mother's lips thinned.

I cast back in my memory for the man's name. Gunther, I thought it was.

The Head Council shook his head and gave me a long-suffering sigh. "I don't know why I ever expect maturity from you, Keeper. I'm fairly sure you don't have any."

I bit the inside of my lip to keep from telling him that respect must be earned. From what I'd seen of the Universal

Council, they were little better than a bunch of bickering toddlers. Knowing that the fate of the Americas might be on their shoulders was terrifying. "I apologize, sir. I've been under a lot of strain lately."

"Yes," he said, seeming to soften. "As have we all. So much so that, despite previous actions that led us to believe you didn't grasp how dangerous the Rune Key is, we're willing to listen to your proposal."

I inclined my head, wishing I *had* a proposal. "Yes, sir."

The room was silent again, all eyes on me. I shifted slightly and twitched as Maddie cleared her throat in a wordless prompt.

"Okay, this is the thought," I said. "These artifacts are a group of toxic magic that nobody knows how to control..."

"We already know that," Fish Face said. "Tell us something we don't know."

I bit back a response that would probably get me a face full of fish spit. "Right. And, at the risk of repeating information you all know, nobody has been able to slow or stop their toxicity." I glanced at the council, letting the truth sink deep.

It was true that I'd been disrespectful. But they'd been overly proud. And in this case at least, they had no grounds for that pride. "Nobody," I repeated, narrowing my eyes.

"If you believe that insulting us all will help plead your case," said the vampire. "You are wildly mistaken."

I flapped a hand. "Sorry. You misunderstand. What I'm trying to point out is the improbability that none of the supernormals in this room or anywhere could solve an artifact issue. Including," I added, "All the Keepers—sorcerers who are intimately connected to thousands of powerful artifacts and manage them every day."

Understanding began to soften scowls behind the dais. I even got a tiny nod from Maddie.

"How likely is that?"

"It's extremely unlikely," the Head Council said. "But those are the facts."

I nodded in agreement. "Exactly. So, I need to ask, why is the Rune Key so dangerous?"

Splutters emerged from half the council.

"It's the most powerful artifact in the universe," said my mother, her tone not hostile.

I looked into her hazel gaze and saw the beginnings of understanding there.

She appeared to be mostly alone in that.

"Girl, get to the point!" the Head Council barked.

"The Rune Key controls all magic. It can unlock any artifact. It gives its handler total control of every type of magic in the universe. In short, it is above control itself. As is this group of toxic artifacts."

"Wait," pig nose said. "The girl might actually be onto something. We've never found a magic the Rune Key couldn't manage."

Heads began to bob. Some of their expressions morphed from disdain to understanding.

And then they began to argue.

I sighed.

Maddie moved closer to the communication mirror in the council chambers and smiled. "You might as well all take a seat," she told all callers. "This will take a while."

"Do you have any idea what their decision will be? I asked the PTB.

She shook her head. "Half of the council wants us to bury the key in the deepest hole we can dig and reinforce the hole with every death-dealing ward we can come up with." She arched a perfectly coiffed eyebrow. "Especially since that stunt you and your people pulled."

I shrugged. "I don't regret it."

"That's only because it didn't blow up in your face. This time it has real potential to end our existence."

I shrugged again. "Fair point." I turned a questioning gaze her way. "But what are our options?"

She didn't respond. But I thought I saw agreement in her expression.

Did I have Madeline Quilleran on my side? I wasn't sure. But if she was, that would help sway several of the council. So much so, they might be willing to take a chance.

They debated for an hour.

So much for a brief meeting.

Then the council dismissed all callers and told us to stay tuned for instructions. I didn't even know what they'd decided. But I had hopes they were going to go with my suggestion.

My question to Maddie had been sincere. I really didn't see any other options.

22

I THOUGHT YOU PEOPLE WOULD NEVER FEED ME

Lea returned to Croakies a couple of hours later. Grym arrived about the same time, and they filed into the bookstore, noses twitching at the delicious aroma of tacos, pizza, and egg rolls.

"Quite the combo," Lea teased as she gave me a hug.

"Well, I figured if the world was ending, we might as well enjoy a last meal of some of our favorite things." I'd meant it to be a joke, but the pitying looks they gave me told me I'd failed miserably.

Grym wrapped an arm around my shoulders and kissed me on the temple. "It's going to be fine. Sebille told me about what Slimy said and I think he's spot on."

"You do?" My question sounded pathetically insecure, but I found that I craved reassurance. I'd have felt better if the council had told me they supported the project.

"I do. It makes perfect sense."

"Great," Lea said. "Now, at the risk of being rude, can we eat? I haven't eaten in almost a day and my insides are gnawing on each other."

"So that was the sound I heard a minute ago," Sebille teased. "I thought somebody was hawking up a hairball."

"Har de har har."

The front door opened six inches and got stuck on the heaved doorjamb. Rustin turned sideways and grunted as he forced his way between the door and the frame. He shook his head when he spotted us. "You started without me?"

Grym didn't even look up as he filled his plate with food. "You bet we started without you. As soon as the hobgoblin and the brownie smell this food, there won't be any left for anybody else."

That got Rustin moving. He shoved between Grym and Lea and I thought I heard growling.

"Lea, stop growling at Rustin."

"He budged!"

Sebille snorted. "Step back, kitty cat, or the witch will bite off your fingers."

"My growl is mightier than yours," Rustin told Lea.

"You'd be wrong if you believe that. I'm hangry. Have you ever dealt with a hangry woman?"

Rustin lost some of the color in his cheeks and he stepped back, lifting his hands in surrender.

I handed him a paper plate. "Just get at the end of the line and nobody will eat your fingers."

He stepped behind Sebille, cutting me from the line.

I growled.

Rustin snatched up a slice of pizza and retreated, leaving us to fill our plates before filling his.

Just as he was stepping up to the table again, the dividing door opened and Hobs flew in, clear blue gaze wide with interest. "Food!"

Rustin dove for the table. But it was too late. In a wash of white cotton air, the hobgoblin cleared everything that was left on the table and disappeared back into the artifact library.

We all stood staring in disbelief as the door slammed closed on the backwash of his departure.

Recovering slightly, I headed for the tea area. Quietly, I pulled another pizza box and bags of tacos and egg rolls out of the niche where we hid stuff we didn't want Hobs to eat. I placed the food on the table and cleared the empties.

Rustin gave me a wide grin. "You're the best."

"Finally!" a large voice boomed as the dividing door opened and the Meister lumbered in. She was wearing basketball shorts and an oversized sweatshirt bearing a logo from Ogre U on the front. Wiry orange hair stuck out from the hem of her shorts and showed in the V-neck of her shirt. "I thought you people would never feed me."

The ogre shoved Rustin out of the way and grabbed the pizza box, stacking the bags of food on top of it. Then she disappeared back through the dividing door, and slammed it behind her.

Rustin looked totally dejected. "Why is she still here, exactly?"

I frowned, not really sure.

"Because nobody wants to tell the king his Rock Meister sucks fuzzy caterpillar cocoon," Sebille said, her cheeks bulging with food.

All heads bobbed in agreement.

Rustin looked so despondent that I tried to recall what food I had upstairs in my apartment. Then I remembered I couldn't get to it anymore. I was staircaseless. Eying Sebille, I wished I had wings.

"I don't know how you two ever get any food around here," Rustin groused, looking miserable.

Sebille rolled her eyes and gave him a half-eaten egg

roll.

Lea came up with half a taco. Grym snorted when he saw Rustin staring at his plate and hunkered protectively over it.

I gave my friend a piece of pizza I'd really been looking forward to eating. Then I remembered that platter of frosted brownies on Hobs' table. Was it possible there were still some left?

It seemed unlikely. But worth a try?

I motioned to Rustin. "Come on, you and I are going on a special mission."

His frown didn't turn upside down as I'd hoped. But he followed without argument. He'd probably been too weak from hunger to do otherwise.

RUSTIN SAT BACK in his seat and belched, rubbing his distended belly and grinning like the Cheshire cat.

Unbelievably, the platter of brownies had been right where I'd seen it earlier. Apparently, Hobs preferred to eat all *our* food before diving into his favorite dessert.

Using the Hawkwarts invisibility cloak artifact I'd recently acquired, we'd managed to sneak up on the food-stealing twosome through Hobs' fully-exposed front door and get hold of the platter.

It hadn't been easy. We'd fallen over boards, caught our toes in divots on the concrete caused by the ceiling and walls crashing to the floor, and I'd bumped my knee against the leg of the table that held the tray of goodies as we reached for it.

Ultimately, it had been Baca who'd sounded the alarm. Somehow, she'd looked right through the invisibility cloak and spotted us hunkering there. Apparently the artifact wasn't brownie-proof.

Good to know.

"Stop thieves!" she'd called, her high-pitched voice filled with glee.

With an indignant squawk, Hobs shot toward us, helped by the fact that we ran into a chair on our way out. But Rustin roared like his alter ego and Hobs squeaked to a stop, shaking like a blade of grass in a wind-storm.

And the rest was history.

"We need to be ready when the counsel tells us it's a go," Rustin said.

I narrowed my eyes at him, pointing to my face to indicate he had a big blob of frosting above his lip.

He licked it off.

"I agree," Sebille said. "Knowing them, they'll expect us to be ready to go the instant they give us the okay."

I knew she was right, but... "All five teams will need to perform the same spell at the same time for this to work," I said. "We'll need to collaborate with the other four teams about what they're doing."

Grym winced. "Speaking as someone whose job requires a lot of meetings and collaboration, that's a really bad idea. That type of thing takes forever. Especially when you're dealing with big egos and a variety of supernormal types. You know how supernormals are," he went on as I opened my mouth to argue. "Every magic type thinks they're the best, the brightest, the most talented of all. By the time we break through the wall of egos, the world will already be ended."

"He's not wrong," said Lea. "That kind of narrow thinking is why I left Corporate America and opened my own little shop."

"So, let's come up with a spell and try to sell it to the council," Sebille suggested. "Let the council shove it down everybody's throats."

"That's not a bad idea," Rustin said. "It will be easier than battling it out with a hundred other supernormals."

"Okay, I said. Let's do it. Does anybody have any ideas for the type of spell we should use?" I looked at Lea. As our resident witch, she was the most likely to have a starter spell we could adjust to create the magic we needed.

She frowned thoughtfully. "The Rune Key makes any spell we create more powerful and effective. That's going to be a lot of power for the teams to control once it's been engaged. The key will hold the center point, at the top of the spell. The five teams will be the spokes leading to the key. Probably our biggest challenge is that our spoke needs to be strong enough to meet the key and then hold together when the entire wheel is engaged."

"So, our first potential breaking point is where our spell meets the key?" Grym asked.

Lea nodded. "And the second breaking point is after all five spokes engage with the key. The power that comes from that joining will be epic. It's something that's never been done before. So, in addition to being epic, it will also be unpredictable."

I wiped suddenly sweaty palms on my jeans. "Okay. That means every spoke needs to be identical in form and, it sounds like, in power."

"Exactly," Lea agreed.

"I'm going to add another layer of complexity to that," Sebille said. "If each spoke needs to be identical, that means identical supernormals on each team. Equal magical strength and maybe equal magical types too."

I groaned, suddenly realizing just how impossible a task

it was that we were taking on. I grabbed the pad and pencil I'd brought to the table and did a sketch with potential weak points and construction points.

"Okay, that's the theory," Grym said. "Now, what about the infrastructure of the spell?"

"That's going to take a bit of brainstorming," Lea said, glancing at Sebille. "The question is, do we want this to be witch-focused, or fae-focused?"

"How about a mix of both?" I asked.

"Off the top of my head?" Sebille said. "Using both would complicate the make-up of the teams across the board. It would mean including both witches and fae of the exact same rank and strength in five different groups. It could be done. But it would take time we don't have. I recommend we decide on one or the other. That's not to say either or both couldn't add magic to the spoke, just that only one should be a focus."

"How are we going to do that?" Grym asked, frowning.

I glanced around at my friends. "We go with witch-based," I said. "Because Enchanted has more powerful witches than anything else."

"The Quillerans," Lea said, nodding. "Maddie's PTB, Maude's super powerful despite how young she is. And Rustin..."

We all looked at him, likely thinking the same thing. He'd give us two powerful supernormals in one.

"Would the Chimera make it difficult to match on the other teams?"

"We'd need to discuss that with Maddie. She might say that we could substitute another ancient magical creature for the Chimera on the other teams. Maybe ancient magic is strong enough to remove the need for an identical match."

I nodded, scribbling "Ancient magic" on my pad.

23

DING DONG THE BELL IS DEAD

The call I'd been subconsciously waiting for came an hour before dawn the next morning. I'd spent a restless night on the floor of the bookstore, tucked in the space between the sales counter and the tea area. It had taken us a while to clear the spot, but it was the farthest from the crevice and therefore deemed the safest.

Sebille had opted to stay in the greenhouse with the fae and their queen, likely planning to run through our potential spell design with her mother, to verify that it was a plausible plan.

I hadn't had to persuade Grym to stay with me, since he was already worried about my staying at Croakies, given the current state of the toxic cleft running through the building.

He'd been as restless as me for most of the night, and we'd spent the midnight hours discussing the problem and coming up with little to improve our initial spell design.

I was making a cup of tea, smiling at Grym's rumbling snores, when the communication mirror in the library chimed. I deserted my tea and hurried through the dividing door. A concussive level of snoring greeted me as I passed through the door, jolting me to an alarmed halt before I realized who it was.

The Rock Meister. Even inside my mind, the title came out in a snarl. The odious creature was draped over a pile of sharp-edged rock and concrete, her thick form not showing any sign of being uncomfortable in her rocky bed.

She'd tried her filigreed rock and alien moss concoction the night before, with mixed results. She'd been able to fill in a three-foot-by-three-foot section of the crevice and it had stayed fixed. But that filled spot hadn't spread to repair the rest. It would take truckloads of the stuff to fix the whole town, which wasn't feasible. And that would do nothing for the other areas being affected by the constantly spreading toxin. So, it hadn't been the answer to our problem.

The communication mirror was rounding the corner in front of the door when I stepped into the library. I sent out a pulse of keeper magic to summon the mirror over, then another pulse to answer the summons as it settled to the debris-strewn floor.

The surface of the mirror swirled with roiling gray fog, the depth of the color deeper at the edges and thinning near the center.

Madeline's slender form appeared as the fog dispersed. She looked exhausted. "Naida keeper. The council has tasked me with giving you their decision, and working with you as we move forward."

My heart thumped faster in my chest. Silver stars burst before my eyes. Madeline's mouth was set in a grim line. Her gaze as it locked onto me, was fierce.

She seemed to be waiting for me to respond. I could barely breathe, so the best I could do was to say, "Okay," the word breathy and broken.

Madeline's eyelids fluttered. I got the impression she'd

wanted to roll her eyes at my mental expansiveness. The PTB sighed. "They agreed to the use of the Rune Key to stop the toxic pentagram magics."

I expelled the breath I'd been holding, so relieved my knees went weak.

"They're working on a spell now. I'll get back to you when they have it."

My knees went rigid and my heart tried to hack a few divots out of my ribs. All I could think about was the constant bickering of the council. They fought about everything. Deciding if they wanted to take a coffee break probably took them an hour. If we waited for them to come up with a spell, the world would be ended and rotted to dust before they finished.

"No!" I said as Madeline stared at me. "That will take too long."

She looked as if she didn't disagree, but she straightened her shoulders and fixed me with a narrow-eyed look. "The Universal Council is the best of the best in the supernormal universe. *Surely*, you don't mean to imply they are incapable of creating one spell?"

The air in front of Maddie sparked with light and Shirley, the ill-tempered pixie appeared.

I watched in fascination, wondering if Shirley would verbally assault the PTB for her word usage. I didn't have to wait long. Shirley took one look at her prospective victim and curtsied, disappearing in a burst of pale light and leaving an apology hanging on the air.

Immediately forgetting the pix, Madeline said, "We'll get back to you," and began to fade away.

"Wait!" I called out before she was completely erased by the swirling shadows in the mirror.

Maddie held up a hand. "What?" She sounded cranky and impatient.

"We've started designing a spell already. Can you get the council to look at our spell once it's done?"

She hesitated only a moment, then asked, "Who is *we*?"

"Lea, Sebille, Rustin, and I..." I hesitated only a beat before adding, "Queen Sindra." I wasn't absolutely sure if Sebille had run it by her mother, but I suspected she had.

"Send it to me when it's done. If I approve, I'll give it to the council."

Did she look relieved by that idea?

I nodded. "We'll get it to you as soon as possible."

She disappeared from the mirror without comment.

"Was that Madeline?" Grym asked as I turned away from the mirror. "Yes," I said. "We need to finalize our spell design tout de suite and send it to her."

His dark brows lifted. "She's agreed to present it to the council?"

"If she approves," I grimaced. "What are the chances she'll approve?"

"Pretty good," Lea said, striding into the room. I gave my bestie a tired smile. "Hey. I didn't hear the bell."

"The bell is dead," Sebille said, buzzing into the library behind Lea. "The crack killed it."

I sighed. "Talk to me," I told Lea. "Why are the chances good that Maddie will approve our spell?"

"Because Mother added an irresistible flourish to it," Sebille said, grinning.

Hope swelled in my heart. "What's the flourish?"

"I'll explain as we create the spell," the sprite said. "Let's get it on paper and send it to Maddie." Her gaze darkened with worry. "Before the greenhouse collapses from the massive crack now running through it."

TWO HOURS LATER, we were putting the finishing touches on the spell, and I felt confident that even the cranky toddlers on the council would appreciate the work we'd done. Would they find flaws in the spell? It was likely. But would they feel compelled to trash the whole thing and start over? Not very likely. Even if they wanted to rework it a bit, we had hopefully carved a few hours...days? weeks?...off the timeframe involved if they'd designed the spell themselves.

I called Maddie and sent our design through the mirror with another pulse of keeper magic.

She accepted it without a word and immediately started reading. The witch didn't react at all, leaving me unable to determine if she thought it would work.

At last, she frowned and looked up. "What's the significance of the fairy knots?"

I grinned. "Queen Sindra suggested them. There are five. One for each element. They're meant to strengthen and add power to the spell."

She nodded thoughtfully, "A spell like this is going to need a massive amount of power to work."

"That's why we're proposing we use the pavilion at Enchanted Park."

"The enhancing structure in the woods." It wasn't a question. It was a recognition of our intent. "That might work. Every team should have access to something similar." She pointed to the detail on spell casters we'd included. "Explain your thinking on these."

I explained what we'd determined as far as giving each team equivalence in casters and power levels. "We're thinking a keeper, three witches or two witches and a fairy, and an ancient power of some kind on each team."

"Five casters for the five elements." Madeline nodded, a smile forming on her face for the first time. "It's good. This just might work."

I smiled too, unable to help myself. "You'll present it to the council?"

"I will. Presume it's going to pass muster with them and get everything ready. If we're going to do this, it should be tonight at midnight. Things are degenerating fast." Her expression darkened again and I nodded. "Yeah. They are."

Madeline started to fade away and stopped. "Maude will be with your team."

I nodded, pleased. "Good." Maude was only nineteen, but she had the innate Quilleran power and had been training under her Aunt Madeline for over a year. She'd be a great addition to the team.

As the mirror fogged completely over, I leaped into the air and screamed with joy. If things went as planned, we could knock the toxic magic into a wormhole in the universe by the wee hours of the morning.

I hurried out of the library and started calling in the team. I could see the end in sight, but we still had a ton of work to do before we could release our spell.

THE MOON WAS ROUND, high, and bright, its fullness flinging silver light across the ground. Hundreds of pretty stars cut into the roof of the pavilion made the moonlight dance like fairy lights across a thick carpet of grass.

Built by supernormals to enhance and supercharge any magic performed beneath its roof, the pavilion had been part of my childhood long before I'd discovered its real purpose. For our purposes that night, it was the perfect tool.

"Twenty-five minutes and thirty-five seconds, people," Sebille barked out. She buzzed over the heads of Lea, Rustin, and Maude as they carefully created the pentagram we'd need to project our spell. They were brushing it with special paint that enhanced the magic just a little bit more, an addition from the council that nobody believed would make a difference, but which we had no choice but to use in the design. The paint had already made us late, being a complex mixture made with hard-to-find ingredients that we'd scoured Enchanted to find. As it was, only sheer luck and a strong knowledge of magical ingredients got us where we needed to be. Even with that, we were twenty-three minutes and thirty seconds away from being too late to join the other four groups when they kicked off the spell we'd designed.

Seemingly oblivious to the tension surrounding them, Vel and Wicked explored the trees at the edge of the woods, happy to be outside.

"Twenty-three minutes."

Rustin growled and snapped his teeth at Sebille as she buzzed overhead.

"Don't snap at me, kitty-cat. I need time to make the fairy knots before we go live."

"Argh!" Lea yelled. "This paint is stiffer than an armadillo's backside."

"And smells like one too," Grym added. He'd been in charge of clearing debris from the roof so the little magical stars were cleared to enhance the magic. He was still on a ladder, despite the fact that he'd already cleared all the stars, because some idiot had jammed a hunk of wood into the pentagonal opening in the very center of the structure. Without that focusing object, our magic would be dispersed in a wave rather than a beam.

We needed maximum control and distance for the beam to reach the rune key that was set up in the Universal Council chambers. We needed that focused beam.

I fought a gentle but steady wind in trying to light the six candles we'd placed—one on each point and one in the center.

"Tell me how this is going to work again," Grym said as he worked. "Shouldn't the key be somewhere out in space? We're going to be directing this beam straight up into the sky."

"The key will form a wheel that connects with all five beams," Lea said. "Putting itself in the center."

He grimaced as he reached inside the hole and fought to loosen the object plugging it. "I'll take your word on that. I'd feel better if I could see it."

"Maybe you will," I told him. "I'm not sure if it will be visible from Earth or not."

"Eighteen minutes, people!"

"Will anybody hate me if I eat the giant, mouthy bug?" Rustin growled.

"I won't!" came a voice out of the darkness.

With a sharp whine, Vel ran out of the trees, fur fluffed and tail tucked. She growled low in her throat and pressed her soft body against my legs, staring toward the spot the voice had come from.

I jerked in surprise and bumped the candle I was trying to light with my knuckles, toppling it.

The barrier in the pentagonal focus came loose without warning and Grym fell backward with the force of his effort, arms flailing and mouth open on a grunt of alarm. He fell off the ladder and crashed to the ground outside, but not before he slammed a hip into the sharp edge of the wooden floor.

"Ah!" Lea glanced in alarm at Grym and reached for him, too late, but the movement jarred the paintbrush in her hand and caused her to slash outside the lines. "No!" she screamed, then jerked downward as Sebille buzzed by too close, spilling fairy dust all over the floor and the still-wet paint.

"Sebille!" Lea screamed, before noticing Sebille was dodging magic bullets coming from somewhere.

"Maude!" Rustin yelled. "What's happening there?"

Her wavy blonde hair flying, the young witch swung her arms and screamed, leaping to her feet and sending bolts of magic wildly around as she slapped at a giant hairy spider that appeared to be clinging to her leg. "Ahhhhh! Get it off me!" Her pretty blue eyes were like saucers in her slender face.

Rustin rose too fast, intending to help, and toppled his dish of paint, creating a giant splotch on the deck that spread quickly toward the pentagram.

Somebody laughed and clapped his hands.

We all turned at once, an array of expressions pointed toward the sound.

To my unending shock, London walked from the shadows. He waved. "Hey, everybody."

"London?" I said, incredulous. "What are you doing here?"

He grinned widely, swiping a thick wave of hair off his face. "I heard magic was happening and I wanted to see. I'm kind of what you'd call a student of magic."

"More like a student of chaos." Maude turned to us. "Why are you guys hanging around with a trickster?"

A...what?

24

TRICKSTERS DO ANSWER TO GARGOYLES

"He's a trickster." Maude turned her glower back toward London. "I thought Aunt Maddie told you to get lost."

London shrugged, a smug smile painting his face. "Tricksters don't listen to witches. You're inferior to us."

Maude lifted her hands, sparks snapping at her fingertips. "I'll give you inferior right up your trickster tuckus."

London laughed. His hands snapped out almost faster than I could follow. Dark, swirling motes filled the air above our pentagram and started to settle onto the paint. As they settled, the paint started to disappear. Even worse, the candles at the points began to melt from the bottom, spreading in a messy glop that I'd be unable to light.

"No!" I yelled. "We don't have time."

London laughed again, the sound bouncing around us like an echo in a cavern. "That's the best time for chaos!"

Maude shot a magical bullet at the trickster. He stepped sideways just before it would have struck him and it sailed across the park, slamming into a copse of mature evergreens instead. Fire bathed the trees, and a thick fog of smoke filled the clearing.

I coughed violently, the smoke stinging my eyes and burning my chest.

"Ten minutes!" Sebille screamed through the miasma, her warning sliced off by violent coughing.

London bent his knees and leaped onto the roof of the pavilion. He extended his hands out to his sides and spread his fingers, thin trails of black sparkles shooting from the tips. The motes hit the roof and ate through its surface, creating round holes where the stars had been.

I crawled over to Sebille, screaming over the roar of the fire and the growl of a building wind. I hadn't even noticed when the wind arrived. "We need to stop him."

"No kidding!" Sebille yelled back. She leaped into the air, turning buggy in the midst of her jump. She disappeared into the smoke and a moment later, streams of pale green magic lit the haze.

I glanced around the pavilion, looking for something I could use against the trickster. There was nothing. Down by my feet, Wicked spun in circles like a dog, chasing his tail. He spit and hissed angrily even as he spun.

"The box!" Lea yelled as rain suddenly pelted us, the attacking drops driven sideways by the roaring wind.

I frowned, not following her.

Sebille suddenly shot from the veil of smoke, moving faster than I'd ever seen her move. A beat later, I saw why. An enormous wasp shot from the smoke behind her, its stinger mere inches from her tiny form.

One sting from a bug that big and she'd be dead.

I panicked, leaping up to block the wasp's attack. Sharp pain, like the insertion of a horse-sized needle, pierced my chest. The wasp reversed course and withdrew its stinger as a burning pain unlike anything I'd ever felt before spread in my chest.

"Five minutes!" Sebille screeched. She popped into human form and sent a jet of power toward the wasp.

London's eerie laughter rose over the wind, rain, and fire sounds.

Sebille dropped to her knees on the ground, coughing violently.

I curled into the fetal position and gasped as wave after wave of pain sliced through me. I felt as if I was dying. "We won't make it," I wheezed out.

Rustin's Chimera galloped toward the trickster and London shot away from him, laughing hysterically. He was faster than light and as agile as wind. The mythical creature roared with frustration, unable to keep up.

London disappeared into the night. A moment later, all our cell phones started to ring. A spark leaped from a nearby tree and found the pavilion, flaring quickly into flame.

Thunder rolled overhead and lightning slammed into the earth, so close all the hair on my body stood on end.

I tried to stand as Sebille yelled, "Three minutes!"

London reappeared much closer than expected. Behind him, the darkness took on shape as a large form appeared.

"Yeow!" Wicked screamed as he threw himself at London. The feline smacked into a barrier and yowled unhappily as he slid toward the ground.

The trickster laughed.

Dirt started to fly as Vel tried to dig her way under London's magical blockage. The trickster squatted down and growled at the little dog, showing even white teeth. When Vel barked unhappily, London cackled in response.

Lea released the spell she'd been crafting, her agile

fingers dancing on the air. It flew across the space between us and London. The magic stopped mere inches from the trickster and curved around him on the front and two sides. The space behind him was open. Frustration filled Lea's expression and she visibly strained to complete the trapping barrier.

London's smile turned smug. "I told you, tricksters don't answer to *witch* magic." He said the word "witch" like it was something nasty, adding insult to injury by winking.

A second spell slammed into Lea's and Maude moved to stand next to her, fingers carving magic on the air as she walked. The barrier shimmied, thickened, but didn't close behind London. He could have walked out of it at any time. That he hadn't done so, was a testament to his arrogance.

Rustin returned to human form and added his power to that of the two witches, sending silvery particles of power to coat the spell they'd already crafted. Once again, the barrier shimmied, seemed to stretch, an inch or two, but then it died, unable to enclose him fully.

"Time for me to go," he called out, waving gaily. London turned and took a step, his barrier dropping.

A massive fist emerged from the shadows and slammed into his smug face. He wobbled, staggered back a step, came up against the barrier the witches had built, and then fell to his knees.

Lea's and Maude's barrier snapped around him.

Grym nodded, his expression satisfied. "I guess Tricksters *do* answer to gargoyles."

"We have a little over a minute," Sebille screamed. "I'm working on the roof. The pentagram is a mess."

Lea, Rustin and Maude went back to the pentagram, working quickly to restore it as best they could.

I shoved to my feet. "I need candles!"

Lea nodded toward the canvas bag she'd brought. "There are some smaller ones in my bag. They'll have to do."

"Bring the pentagram on line a point at a time," Sebille called out. "I need to build fairy knots."

Nodding, the witches did as requested, working frantically to redraw the magically corroded pentagram.

I hurried to Lea's bag and dug out six white candles. They were half the size of the other ones and I prayed they'd be enough.

"Spirit's online," Lea called.

I hurried over and placed a candle on Spirit, lighting the wick as quickly as I could. It helped that the wind had died and the rain no longer pelted us.

"Wind's online," Maude called. I placed a candle on the wind point and lit it.

Sebille buzzed frantically from one point to the next, leaving behind glittering fairy knots that hung above each point.

"Water's online!" Rustin screamed.

"I've got earth online," Maude yelled.

I scurried around, placing my candles as quickly as I could.

"Twenty seconds," Sebille called.

"Air's on!" Lea screamed.

High above our heads, golden light speared the sky. One stream. Two streams. Three.

"Ten seconds!" Sebille yelled as another fairy knot flared to life.

Four streams.

The four magical streams seemed to hang in the air, pulsing impatiently as they waited for us. My heart rocked inside my chest. My stomach twisted. We weren't going to make it. After everything that had happened. We were going to fail.

The last knot flared to life.

"Points!" Maude screamed.

We all took our spots, arms outstretched, and started to chant.

We come together magically, to heal the poison we set free. Save the spirit, let it be. In dire need we call the key.

We come together magically, to heal the poison we set free, Save the air, let it be. In dire need we call the key.

We come together magically, to heal the poison we set free, Save the fire, let it be. In dire need we call the key.

We come together magically, to heal the poison we set free, Save the earth, let it be. In dire need we call the key.

We come together magically, to heal the poison we set free, Save the water, let it be. In dire need we call the key.

As the final words of our chant left our lips, we all stared helplessly toward the four glowing threads of magic high above our heads. As I watched them pulse accusingly, a knot of pure fear ached in my middle.

We'd failed. We'd failed Enchanted and everyone else. *I'd* failed. I should have been better. I should have *done* better.

I should have…

Our pentagram burst into light, the energy spreading across the ceiling and focusing into the pentagular opening in the center. The glittering stream of golden magic shot up to meet the others and I swore I could hear the collective howl of success from across the world.

We sent up our own cheer, our eyes straying only briefly from the phenomenon above us as we grinned around the circle.

We fell silent. Waiting. Watching. We weren't done yet.

The threads of magic pulsed harder, seemingly growing more erratic as the seconds ticked slowly by.

My heartbeats formed around the magic's pulse, matching its rhythm.

A warm arm found my shoulders. Soft, cool fingers wrapped around mine. A familiar buzzing sound gave me comfort as Sebille joined Grym and Lea in silent support.

The key hadn't appeared.

"It didn't work," I whispered. "The key's not there."

"Give it time," Maude said.

I swung a brief look in her direction. She and Rustin stood nearby with linked arms and hopeful faces.

Something glimmered at the juncture of all the spokes. A shadow formed there. The spokes moved.

"Something's happening," Grym said, his arm tightening around me.

Illumination flared at the junction of the spokes and a round golden circle was suddenly there. The circle began to spin as magic shivered down the spikes, amping them up until we were squinting against the light.

"The key!" Maude yelled. She pointed, bouncing on her toes and clapping her hands with excitement. "It's there!"

The shape was unlike any key I'd ever seen. It wasn't a key, but a circle with strands of silver, green, and purple striping its surface. Forged within the strands were a variety of rectangular shapes, which could have resembled the teeth of an old-fashioned key.

The magical artifact started to spin at the end of the spokes. Its rotations increasing in speed until it was a blur of light that shimmied down the spokes and dripped off the perimeter of the key.

Then the spokes started to spin. As they rotated, they grew and pulsed, flaring outward from each other and creating a revolving wheel in the sky. An explosion of blinding white light burst through the darkness. When it was gone, so was the key. But magic sifted downward, bathing the night in light and a rainbow of colors that represented the supernormals who'd spun the spell.

When the magic landed on me it felt cool, zinging with positive magical energy.

Enchanted City lit with the magic. All the damage the trickster had done repaired itself. I felt rather than saw the earth knitting itself back together beneath our feet. And I knew, in that moment, that the spell we'd made worked.

A collective scream of delight shattered the silence of the park, and I threw myself into my friends' enthusiastic hugs.

Against all odds, we'd done it.

25

I CALL IT THE KRAZY KEEPER

I tucked the prison minimizing box into the toxic magic vault and closed the door, spinning the special locks so that only Sebille or I could open the door. I'd realized, too late, that Lea had been calling for me to trap the trickster in a prison box when we'd been battling him in the park.

The realization made me feel stupid. But I pushed the feeling away. I wasn't perfect. And better late than never. An unhappy, minimized trickster was nestled safely inside the box, awaiting the arrival of a representative from Casa De Grimoire, the supernormal prison system.

I lingered in the artifact library for a moment before returning to my friends in the bookstore. A smile found my face as I looked at the repaired shelves and the reshelved artifacts. The floor and walls were blemish free, and the stairs to my apartment were back in place and whole again.

Even the wall separating Hobs' little piece of heaven in a different dimension from earth was back in place. I smiled at the large sign tacked on the wall where the new wall was. It read,

No brownie thieves welcome!

Irony at its best.

My smile widening, I hurried over to Shakespeare's desk and dug through the drawers for a piece of paper and a permanent marker. Scribbling a quick message on the paper, I taped it to the dividing door and stepped back, grinning.

It read:

Thieves of ANY kind of food not welcome.

I opened the door and stepped into a party.

The spicy aroma of our favorite foods assailed me and my mouth watered. I started across the room and Grym turned with a smile. He held an arm open for me to walk into.

Lea handed me a plate and kissed me on the cheek. Sebille rolled her eyes and shoved between me and the dessert area.

Seeing it, I nearly groaned under the rich scent of moist chocolate brownies. My salivary glands kicked into overdrive and I nearly shoved past Sebille so I could snatch a brownie...or two.

Rustin was sitting on the floor next to Slimy's tank and the little squish was happily sunning himself on his heated rock. I wiggled a finger at the frog. *You feeling better?*

I'm perfection in a waterproof green skin.

I'll be the judge of that, said an unfamiliar voice. I blinked, realizing there was another occupant in the tank. A very large occupant. "Wally?"

Lea bumped my shoulder with her own. "He wanted to see his pal and make sure Slimy was okay."

"You didn't tell me he was...talking."

Lea gave me a flat look. "What? I neglected to tell you my bullfrog was talking? How could that have happened? I've just been sitting around with my feet up munching bon bons. How silly of me to forget."

I sighed. "Okay, okay. I get it." I grinned. "That's pretty cool, though. Now the boys can have philosophical discussions together and leave me out of it."

The frog snorted. *Fat chance. Wally's idea of philosophy is a discussion about whether the Colts football team functions best in their white uniforms or the blue.*

Hey, brah! Color is emotion. Especially when you add the location element. There are all kinds of feelings tied to seeing a sports team in its home darks versus away lights. And did you know that some teams choose dark uniforms for away games and light for home. My mind is boggling here. Bawump!

The front door opened and the little bell jangled musically. It made me smile, which told me better than anything that I was exhausted. The woman who walked into the bookstore made my pulse race and eyes go wide. All weariness fled me as I greeted Madeline Quilleran.

The PTB's weary gaze slid toward the food but she looked away as if not interested. Her niece didn't share her indifference. Maude trooped in behind her and squealed, all but running toward the table full of food. "I'm starving. Thanks for doing this, whoever it was."

"You're welcome," Sebille and Rustin said at the same time.

Grym raised a hand. "I did the desserts."

"That's why I love you," I told him.

He winked.

I glanced at Maddie and my smile slid away. "Is everything okay?" I asked her, still not willing to totally believe we'd beaten the toxic magic.

"Yes. All five toxic artifacts have been eradicated. The

key handled them with ease." She fixed her gaze on me. "That was inspired, Naida. Good job."

I flushed with pleasure. "It wasn't me. It was Slimy."

The frog bounced in his tank, smashing his face against the glass.

Maddie nodded at him. "Yes, he's a very smart frog."

If frogs could look smug, Slimy was perfecting the look.

"I actually came to take charge of the trickster."

"Ah."

Sebille threw her empty plate in the trash. "I'll go get him."

"Thanks," I said. I cocked my head at the PTB. "Maude said you'd dealt with him before tonight. What's the story there?"

Maude handed her aunt a plate full of pizza, egg rolls and brownies. Maddie's lips curved slightly. I wasn't sure if it was the food choices or the story about the trickster that caused the smile. "I haven't eaten like this since college," she said.

I flushed with embarrassment. "Sorry. We have basic food tastes around here."

She shook her head and took a bite of an egg roll. Her eyes closed. "Don't apologize. I subsist mostly on salads. This is a little bit of heaven." She swallowed. "The best part is that I can blame you and not feel guilty."

"Always happy to help," I said dryly.

"Can I ask, Naida, how did you meet up with the trickster?"

I told her about the meeting in the forest and the subsequent episodes at the zoo. As I told her the story, I realized the clues had all been there and I hadn't known to look for them. Everything London had touched had gone nipples up. I should have known all that negativity couldn't have happened naturally. "Is he the cause of the toxic pentagram artifacts getting loose in the first place?"

"We believe so. We're not certain, but we believe he turned himself into a cat and stole the artifacts from the universal vault. Leonare was in charge of the vault that day and...well...she thought nothing of letting him accompany her inside. She has a thing for cats." Maddie frowned. "Which is weird because cats eat fish."

I nodded. "Ah. The fish lady. Yeah." My grin might have been a bit smug.

"Right. The trickster made an appearance at every one of the five sites after he released the relics, wreaking havoc and making it impossible for us to succeed. If he hadn't been a factor, we might have defeated the toxic artifacts more quickly and saved lives and property." Maddie frowned, placing an elegant hand over her flat belly. She seemed to have lost her appetite. It made me wonder who she lost in the fight with the artifacts.

The dividing door slammed open and a seven-foot-tall orange-haired vision in a belly-baring yellow tee shirt and poop-brown cargo pants sauntered into the room.

The Rock Meister spotted the food and plowed through the others to get to it. "I can't believe nobody told me there was food. I've been quietly starving upstairs. I'll be telling King Rhorr how you mistreated me. Especially after I solved the fissure issue."

Say that five times real fast, Wally said, chuckling.

"You...what?" I stuttered. The Meister hadn't solved squat. Plus, I was afraid to see what she'd done to my room.

The Meister glanced at Maddie. "You come to congratulate me on my genius fissure fix?"

Say that five times real fast too, Wally added. *Bawump!*

I looked at Lea. "Does that have an off switch?"

She shrugged. "Not that I've found. And believe me, I've looked."

Stop burbling frog, Slimy said. *You're making the natives restless.*

"My fissure fix?" Aelice repeated when Maddie just looked at her. "Remember the filigreed rock and the alien moss? When you all *finally* got them to me, I filled the fracture and sent my special magic into it. The skies opened up and an explosion of magic rained down on it, and the crack was cured. I'm a genius."

"That's the story you're going with?" I asked dryly?

ATA winced. "Do you think King Rhorr will buy it?"

I shrugged.

The ogre is annoyingly alliterative, Slimy said.

Redundantly repetitive, Wally agreed.

"Great," Grym groused. "We've got two of them now."

I sighed.

Sebille entered the bookstore with the prison box and, shortly afterward, the Quillerans left.

Wicked wrapped himself around me, purring loudly. I scooped him up and buried my face in his sweet-smelling fur. "Hey, buddy. You okay?"

"Meow," he told me plaintively.

A whir of white cotton entered the room, shot toward the table, and then halted, morphing into a blue-eyed hobgoblin with an outstretched hand. Hobs stood on a chair since he was too short. His twenty-eight(ish)-inches-tall form couldn't reach the plates from the floor. His long fingers curved like claws over the brownie plate. But he couldn't grasp one.

I grinned. "Problem, Hobs?"

He turned wide blue eyes my way. "Miss, what have you done?"

"I've done what you've done. You put a sign on your door to keep..." I made quotation marks on the air. "... brownie thieves out of your house. I did the same. Unfortunately for you, when the Keeper of the Artifacts creates a rule in the artifact warehouse, the rule has the force of magic."

"But, Miss..."

"You've been running roughshod over everyone for months. Eating everything in Croakies. Not caring if anyone else got food. That ends now. Do you understand?"

A petulant look briefly crossed his face and then fell away under his natural good humor. He smiled. "I'm sorry, Miss. I won't do that anymore."

"Do I have your word? And, before you answer, remember a hobgoblin's word is his bond."

"Yes, Miss. You have my word."

"That's good to hear," Grym said. He walked over and plucked two brownies off the platter, two egg rolls, and two slices of pizza. He arranged everything onto one paper plate and handed it to Hobs. "That's enough for you and the brownie. Bon Appétit."

Hobs looked down at the food on the plate and frowned. "Is this all?"

"If you're still hungry after you eat that, you can have seconds. A normal portion," Grym said with finality.

Hobs sighed and was gone in a blur.

The bell jangled again and I looked up, tensing as I spotted a familiar group coming through the door.

I swallowed hard, wanting to scream out that no bloodshed was necessary.

Seeing the panic on my face, Grym took my hand. "Come on. I'll back you up."

Queen Kaith narrowed her gaze on Grym as we

approached. The queen's guards moved closer to her, their hands resting on the hilts of their swords.

"Queen Kaith," I said by way of a greeting. "Did you come to tell me your queendom is back to normal?" My question was meant to remind her that she no longer had a reason to pick a fight. Judging by the way her jaw tightened, I didn't think she took it well.

"Naida keeper. Yes. My queendom is back in order. It's a good thing I encouraged you to call in the council. Left to your own devices, the whole country would have fallen into the ocean."

I ground my teeth, my lips tightening into a thin line.

"Actually," Grym said, his voice pleasant. "The fix was a joint effort between about a hundred supernormals. It was a unique attempt to join forces between groups, and it was very effective."

Lea stepped up beside me, linking her arm through mine, "We learned it was much better to work together than to always be at cross purposes."

Kaith's expression turned sourer by the moment.

Sebille and Rustin stepped up beside us and the guards wrapped their hands around their sword hilts, partially drawing them.

The queen stared at me for a long moment. Tension filled the room.

Are those trolls? Wally asked in his outside voice. *They suck puffer fish.*

Shhhh! Slimy hissed. *You're projecting to everyone, derf.*

I put a hand over my face and then realized how that would look and pretended I had an itch.

To my surprise, when I looked back at the queen, she was smiling. "We do love puffer fish," she agreed. "It's that element of danger that we crave."

"I can give her danger," Rustin murmured.

I threw him a glare.

"In fact," the queen went on, "We're adding puffer fish to the Thanksgiving menu tomorrow night. That's why I'm here. To invite you to dinner. I hope you like fish?" She turned toward the door before I could answer, leaving me flapping my lips like the above-mentioned puffer. "Um, I don't."

Queen Kaith stopped at the door. "I like the idea of working together. Let me be the first to extend the olive branch. Join me for Thanksgiving dinner, Naida keeper." She looked around at the group. "Bring your friends. The more the merrier. Seven O'clock sharp. Don't be late."

She said that last with a warning growl in her voice. "Ta, ta."

I sagged in horror as the door closed behind them. "We're all going to die for Thanksgiving."

That's not much to be thankful for, Wally said.

True dat, sayeth the frog.

Sebille scurried over to the sales counter and grabbed a notebook. Perched on the tall stool behind the counter, she started happily writing.

"What is that?" I demanded. It seemed I had very little control over my life in general. I'd get control over the stuff that happened under my own roof if it killed me. Like the upcoming dinner would undoubtedly do.

The sprite looked up at me and smiled. "It's for my blog. I call it The Krazy Keeper: How to be a better Artifact Wrangler without the pain of making your own mistakes. I'm writing down every mess you make for yourself and posting it online. My followers are loving it. Danger, intrigue, humor, and certain death. It's great stuff."

Forgetting to swallow for a few beats, I choked on my own spit and had a coughing fit. "You..." *Cheh. Cheh.*

"You posted..." *Cheh. Cheh. Cheh.*

"Online. Yep. I have ten thousand followers already. I'm thinking of starting a podcast. You wouldn't mind if I followed you around with my phone, taping your misery, would you?"

"Ah!" *Cheh. Cheh. Cheh. Cheh.*

That sounds like a great podcast, Wally said. *I'd totally watch that.*

Good luck getting Lea to download it for you, Slimy said.

Why not?

Because they're friends, derf. Now pipe down. Naida's turning green. I think we're going to have to call Doctor Whom.

Cheh. Cheh. Cheh. Cheh.

It ain't easy bein' green, Wally agreed.

The End

DON'T MISS OUT

Stay up on all Sam's news by joining her newsletter, and get a copy of a fun mystery just for signing up!

SIGN UP HERE!
https://samcheever.com/newsletter/

READ MORE ENCHANTING INQUIRIES

If you enjoyed **Cracked Croakies**, you might want to check out the rest of the series: https://samcheever.com/books/ #enchanting

Enjoy this taste of Book 16: Super Croakies:

～

Well, this is just SUPER! Who knew that one little superhero costume could cause so much trouble?

One minute I'm following the trail of a stolen artifact that might have been used for murder at a costume company, and the next I'm chasing an evil supervillain and an enchanted car around town. And to make things worse, apparently the cat and the frog are on the beach. How is that possible? Enchanted doesn't have a beach!

SUPER CROAKIES

S'More Than it Seems

"What in the magical universe is that?" I asked the sprite.

Intensely focused on the pursuit of a perfectly toasted marshmallow, Sebille barely glanced up at the symbol lighting the night sky before shrugging mutely.

The outline of what looked like a hot pink hummingbird hung in the night sky for a moment, and then disappeared in the blink of an eye. "I'm losing my mind," I mumbled.

The night swirled with a soft hiss and two small creatures appeared next to me. "Did you see that, miss?" Hobs asked, his pale blue eyes wide with excitement. The tiny creature standing next to him dressed in shades of brown from head to toe, was staring up at the sky with a perplexed expression. Baca's brown eyes were wide under a pretty headband made of flowers, and her tiny fingers toyed with the tool belt around her waist. "It was really her, wasn't it?"

Sebille placed a finished s'more on the plate warming by the fire. Shoving a long red braid out of her face, she finally focused in on the conversation. "Her who? What did you see?"

I lifted a brow.

"What?" she asked, oblivious.

"That thing in the sky I just called your attention to?"

Her face folded into a frown. "The bird? So what?"

I pulled my shoulder-length brown hair over my shoulder and rolled my blue eyes so hard they bumped against my skull. "It flashed in the sky like a bat signal."

Baca, who was generally a quiet, shy little creature as most brownies were, put her hands on her hips and glared at me. "The Winged Guardian is *not* a bat. She's much cooler than that."

"Isn't that a television show?" Sebille asked. Eyeing the plate of s'mores that held half the number of treats it had a second earlier, the sprite still seemed half distracted. She skimmed a narrow-eyed look toward the hobgoblin standing next to me. Hobs was the picture of innocence, despite the glob of marshmallow decorating his lips.

Fighting a grin, I said, "I wonder if they're taping an episode of the show nearby."

Baca took a bite of s'more, chewing and swallowing before shaking her head. "They just wrapped season two of the new format." She sighed. "It was icy."

How in the world had the brownie gotten hold of the gooey treat? I hadn't even seen her move. A quick look at the nearly empty s'mores plate had me snorting. "I don't know how you two do that, but I want you to teach me."

Hobs winked a pale blue eye, the little tuft of light brown hair bobbing happily between his ears. "The Winged Guardian is much more than a show, Miss Sebille. She's a hero."

Baca nodded enthusiastically. "A superhero. She's a role model for young women everywhere."

I peered into the brownie's tiny face, noting the slightly fanatical glint in her pretty brown eyes. "What's with the bat ... um ... symbol in the sky?"

"Clearly she's pursuing evildoers," Baca said with more than a titch of smugness.

"She's right," Hobs said. Though his agreement with the tiny brownie wasn't unusual since he was totally smitten with her, Hobs seemed particularly certain of the statement. "The bird signal only shows when the Winged Guardian is hunting a villain."

The s'mores plate was suspiciously full again. I slid the sprite a look and she gave me back blank face, but there was a light dancing in her bright green eyes that hadn't been there before.

A beat later, as Sebille slid marshmallows onto the stick she was using to brown them, a soft clanging sound erupted into the peaceful night.

"Ow!" Hobs said, shaking his long-fingered hand, the knuckles of which were purple and already swelling.

"Sebille!" I scolded, horrified. "What did you do?"

"Don't get your bloomers in a twist, Naida. It's just a barrier spell. His hand will be fine." She sniffed pointedly. "That'll teach the little thief to steal from me."

The plate clattered to the ground next to the firepit as the tiny thieves disappeared in a rush, leaving behind only a soft chorus of delighted giggling.

"Troll boogers!" Sebille exclaimed, looking down at the empty plate in the grass. "How do they do that?"

Fighting a grin, I shrugged. "Why do you care? It's just an excuse to make more. You know you love making them."

She couldn't argue, because I was right, so she just

sighed and reached for another marshmallow. Her hand swiped empty air. "Ah!" she shrieked.

The little monsters had taken all the makings too.

She'd really taught *them* a lesson.

My cell rang as I was making breakfast the next morning. It was my boyfriend, aka Detective Wise Grym, aka Grym, because no woman in her right mind would call her boyfriend Wise. That's just asking for trouble. "Hey," I said warmly. "You missed out on one or two stellar s'mores last night."

"Only one or two?" he asked, his deep voice teasing.

"If you were lucky. The hobgoblin and the brownie made an unplanned visit. Amazingly, when they left, all the s'mores and fixings were gone too."

Grym chuckled. "That's a tragedy. Did Sebille launch into the stratosphere? I know how much she was looking forward to making them."

"Let's just say her feet left the ground, and she wasn't wearing her wings." My assistant ... and ... yes ... friend ... was a sprite, with a smaller winged form that came in handy for getting her out of challenging spots. Unfortunately, it hadn't helped her hang onto those s'mores.

"Would a couple dozen doughnuts make it all better?"

My stomach gurgled happily at the thought. "You know it would. But I'm suspicious about your motives."

"Why, Naida Griffith. I'm crushed."

"Since you're mostly rock, that would make you gravel." My sweet and sexy boyfriend was a gargoyle at heart ... and at his magical core. He was heavy on the heavy and darn near indestructible. As a cop in the Supernormal Division, his magical persona came in very useful, and it pretty much explained his driving desire to protect and serve. "But you have an ulterior motive, right?"

"Maybe a small one. I'll see you in fifteen minutes."

I was doing dishes in my apartment when the bell on the bookstore door sounded. Though I lived on the second level, adjacent to the store, I had a magical security ward that warned me whenever anyone entered the shop. I didn't hurry, knowing that Sebille was manning the shop. But my steps might have been lighter than usual, knowing the dual delights of boyfriend and doughnuts awaited my arrival.

I wouldn't have been nearly as excited if I'd known the rest of the household ... prodigious eaters all ... would beat me to the goodies. I sagged unhappily as I eyed the box. All they'd left me was a sad, half-chewed rind of a powdered sugar doughnut.

Grym was standing in the middle of the room, looking gobsmacked. At around six feet tall, with broad shoulders and mahogany hair gilded by sun-kissed streaks, he was a sight for sore eyes. At the moment, though, Grym looked as if someone had beaten him about the head and shoulders with a powdered-sugar-covered pillow. He stood staring into the empty box, his expression shocked.

I sagged. "By the goddess's granny panties, is it too much to ask that you all leave me one doughnut?"

Grym's lips curved and he extended a hand, opening it to show what I thought were probably two doughnuts, slightly mashed together. "I risked losing a few fingers to save you some," he said.

With a shout of pure glee, I threw myself at him and covered his handsome face with kisses. "You see, this is why I love you."

Grym's grin widened. "Nice try. I know you're just

sucking the powdered sugar off my face." The air swirled, and Grym twitched as the crushed doughnuts in his big hand disappeared into thin air.

"Hobs!" I growled out. "You'd better give those back."

A wash of white flashed past and Grym looked down at a chewed ball of doughnut, glossy with spit, resting in his palm. "Ugh." He dumped the chewed pastry into the box and wiped his hand on his jeans. "Don't you ever feed that hobgoblin?"

"Constantly. It's impossible to fill him up," I groused. "He burns too many calories flying around stealing things."

Sebille came around the short wall that dissected the tea counter from the bookstore, a steaming cup of tea in her hand. "You have to be fast around here, Detective," she said, wiping powdered sugar off her lips.

He eyed her with an accusing glare. "I see *you* were fast enough."

The sprite gave him an arch smile. "Always." She reached into her pocket and pulled out a plastic container with a lid, lowering her voice. "Brownies. Shhh."

I snatched the container and held it against my chest, one finger pressed to my lips. I started to open it, and it made a distinctive cracking noise. We all went very still, looking expectantly around.

Fortunately, no brownies or hobgoblins did a road-runner into the room. I glanced at Sebille. She sighed, swirled a finger clockwise, and loud music filled the air. No. I wouldn't call it music. It sounded like people digging through a junkyard, with all the clanking, clanging, grinding, and banging the activity would entail.

I carefully pulled the container open and then got momentarily distracted by Grym swinging his hips to the noise. I barked out a laugh. A soft, brownie-scented breeze wafted over me and there was a tug against my fingertips. When I dragged my gaze from my dancing boyfriend, I discovered my hand was empty again.

"Goddess in a girdle!" I exclaimed loudly.

Sebille made a grab for the container and missed, growling her rage. "Naida!"

My eyes went wide. "Why are you blaming me?"

Sebille swirled a finger counterclockwise and the noise went away. "Because you hesitated. You can't hesitate. They can smell sweets on the air."

Dual giggling drifted toward us from somewhere above our heads.

I sagged. "I'm going to starve to death."

"It's your own fault," the sprite said. Her voice was filled with irritation. Her crabbiness wasn't unusual, but it stirred up guilt where usually I just sloughed it off. "You need to put your foot down with them." She raised her voice, directing her next words to the twittering twosome lurking at the top of the bookshelves. "You need to tell them if they don't stop stealing everybody else's food, they're going to be evicted. We'll see how many sweets they get when they're living on the streets."

I glared at my assistant. "Sebille!"

Silence followed my objection. Her barb had clearly hit home. Half of me was glad *she'd* said it instead of me. I knew it was cowardly, but the twosome had been getting worse over the last few days. It had been so bad that nobody but them had been able to eat. We'd had to resort to dire measures to get any food at all. Apparently, our recent adventure "liberating" a dangerous magical artifact from the Universal Vault to save the fairies had awakened larcenous proclivities in Hobs that had also infected Baca, turning theft into a game they unfortunately excelled at.

"Nobody's getting evicted," I said loudly. Though I shrank under Sebille's growl.

The bell on the front door jangled, and a tall man wearing a brown trench coat and a straw Panama hat came inside. I gave him what was probably a strained smile. "Hello. Welcome to Croakies."

"Hello," he responded, his voice soft and husky. "I'd just like to look around, if I may." His gaze, shadowed by the strange hat, slid over our intense little group.

"Of course."

Sebille dismissed the customer with a quick glance and turned her frown back to me.

The man disappeared into the stacks and we resumed our conversation, voices lowered.

"I came over to ask for your help, Naida," Grym said, throwing the sprite a glare. "Can I borrow your expertise for a while?"

"What's going on?" I asked, feeling a little nauseous from hunger.

Probably totally my imagination.

"I'm not sure," he admitted, offering me his hand. "There was an incident at Regalia and Finery on South Main."

"Incident?" Sebille repeated, frowning. "What kind of incident?"

Grym's dark-caramel gaze was serious. "The deadly kind."

"You think an artifact was involved?" I asked.

He nodded. "From the owner's description, I think it has to be an artifact."

"Okay," I said, taking his hand and allowing him to tug me toward the door. "But I need to eat first. I'm feeling dizzy."

Sebille snorted. "Did your body forget how to forage for calories in your abundant booty?"

"That was mean," I said. "But unfortunately, accurate. For me, calories are like the Hotel California. They can go in, but they can never leave."

Sebille snorted. "Bring me lunch?"

"Done," Grym said, throwing a frown toward the top of the bookshelves. "But I'm not bringing it inside. You'll have to eat it in my car."

Sebille's long-suffering sigh followed us out the door.

Get your copy here: https://samcheever.com/books/

ALSO BY SAM CHEEVER

If you enjoyed **Cracked Croakies,** you might also enjoy these other fun mystery series by Sam. To find out more, visit the **BOOKS** page at www.samcheever.com:

Enchanting Inquiries Paranormal Mysteries - **For more fun adventures with Naida, Sebille, and Wicked!**

Mature Magic Paranormal Women's Fiction

Midlife Muddle Paranormal Women's Fiction

Reluctant Familiar Paranormal Mysteries

Yesterday's Paranormal Mysteries

Gainfully Employed Mysteries

Silver Hills Cozy Mysteries

Country Cousin Mysteries

And More...

ABOUT THE AUTHOR

USA Today and WSJ Bestselling Author Sam Cheever writes contemporary and paranormal mystery and suspense, creating stories that draw you in and keep you eagerly turning pages. Known for writing great characters, snappy dialogue, and unique and exhilarating stories, Sam is the award-winning author of 100+ books.

To learn more about Sam and her work, visit her at one of her online hotspots:

www.samcheever.com

samcheever@samcheever.com